Nuke Them Till Eternity

An Autobiographical novel

Dr. Giora Ram

IMEXCO General
Publishing
Israel

Nuke Them Till Eternity

An Autobiographical novel

Dr. Giora Ram

Copyright © 2010, 2018 by the Author

First published in Israel by IMEXCO General Ltd.,
Titled: "The Hungarian Connection" [2010]

This book is second edition.

ISBN 978-965-91623-9-0

http://nuke.imexco.com

"A hidden connection is stronger than

an obvious one"...

Heraclitus of Ephesus (c. 535-475 BCE)

Dedicated to Israel

and

To those who lived and died

serving and protecting the country.

Table of Contents

1. The Escape from Hungary.

IT WAS A COLD NIGHT; a typical Hungarian winter of 1949 and it had been snowing heavily for the last two days.

The narrow road near the Austro-Hungarian border was covered with snow as were the few naked trees, which looked like giant monsters.

It was quite dark, but the moonlight along with some light from the few houses nearby contributed to the visibility. The air was cold and crisp and a shower of large snow-flakes fell quietly, covering the entire area with a beautiful white carpet.

"Poor kids," Esther said shivering.

"Keep quiet Etelka."

She was hushed by Alex, her husband, who was the group leader. He was carrying his two-year-old son, strapped on his back. He called his wife Etelka, a Hungarian nickname for Ethel or Esther.

They had been driven to the Szombathely area by Alex's friend Jacob, a dealer of second hand items, who owned an old van.

They all met Jacob for the first time at Alex's house before leaving. He dropped them off just a few miles from the border as planned. It was a narrow road and they had to cross the fields on foot to reach the right crossing point.

"Send me a postcard from Vienna," Jacob said, eager to leave and get back to Budapest.

"Will do," said Alex. They hugged briefly and it was clear that Jacob couldn't hide his feelings about the entire scenario. He restarted his van, turned around and drove quietly off.

Alex had learned only a few days ago that Esther was pregnant, and he was worried about the difficulties she might encounter on this journey. At the same time he was also very proud of her being so decisive about the escape.

He thought to himself that after what she had gone through during the war, she must be very strong physically and emotionally.

Esther was in her fifth week of the first trimester. At this stage the baby's central nervous system, the brain and spinal cord, muscle and bone formation are beginning to take shape. During this time, the baby's skeleton is also starting to form.

It was still too early for her to start showing. She felt a bit fatigued, which was common at this stage of the pregnancy.

"It's now or never," she told him when her pregnancy was confirmed.

She knew that as time passed, it would be more and more difficult to leave Hungary.

There were eight adults and five children in the group. All were dressed in layers of clothing, and were carrying cases. Their footprints marked their passing in the deep soft snow.

There was blond Ilona with her grumpy husband Lajos and their children, Michael and Eva. They were the Weisz family.

Ilona was much younger than her husband and one might wonder what made her choose this man, when it was obvious she could have found a better one.

Lajos was very talkative, too much so… and Alex told him several times to keep his thoughts to himself.

In Hungarian the words used were not so politically correct…

The boy, Michael, was about twelve, but seemed older, holding his mother's hand and walking without any complaints, unlike his father, but it was obvious that he was very nervous. Lajos was carrying their three year old daughter, Eva, who slept most of the way.

Katy and Imre Rubinstein, the oldest in the group, were accompanied by their prima-donna daughter, Marika. They had come from Debrecen, the capital of Hajdú-Bihar County east of Budapest and stayed in Budapest for a couple of days until they received the green-light to join the group.

Imre was proud of his teenage daughter in spite of her behavior. Katy, his wife was a beautiful tall classic Slavic looking lady who had raised their daughter in a strict and disciplined manner.

Agi and Mihaly Klein were the last couple to join the group. They had many reservations about leaving Hungarian territory this way. Their nine year old son Pista was not enthusiastic about leaving his friends behind and simply couldn't understand why they were going.

"I want to stay here with Uncle Leo," repeated little Pista.

"I don't want to live with camels and wear a sheet."

He got his impression of life in Palestine from magazines showing life in the Middle-East.

"If you are a good boy you won't have to," Agi said, smiling.

Uncle Leo was a frequent visitor at the Kleins and always brought presents for all the family. No wonder Pista liked him so much.

"We must rest for a while," Lajos said, "it is simply impossible to continue in this weather; my daughter is freezing and my legs are numb."

"Until now everything has gone well, as planned, but we still have the difficult part ahead of us," Alex said in his baritone voice.

"We must proceed immediately as quickly and quietly as possible."

"Alex! We are all tired. How far are we?" asked Imre.

"We have less than one kilometer and we'll be crossing the border into Austria. There is a friend waiting to drive us to Vienna and from there to freedom-to Palestine."

"Do you think we'll make it?"

"The guard at the border was well paid, so I don't expect any problems."

"The previous transport went smoothly. We sent our two older kids ahead and they are safe," Alex replied, breathing heavily, moving again, followed by Imre and the others.

"We must be at Szombathely crossing before the guards' shift change takes place. You know that," said Alex impatiently.
Szombathely was a small city next to the Austrian border. "Szombat" means "Saturday" and "hely," spelled "hey," means "place."

It is the oldest city in Hungary, dating back to medieval times. Markets were held there on Saturdays. Hungary's first Jewish elementary school was founded there in 1846. Most of Szombathely's Jews were deported by the Hungarian authorities to Auschwitz in 1944.

"You can see the light on the horizon. At this pace we'll be there in less than twenty minutes," said Alex, who knew this route from previous successful crossings.

2. Alex and World War II.

ALEXANDER-SHLOMO was born on June 10, 1907 to Hanna-Haya, (1876-1945) and Fülöp-Pinchas (1875-1940) Weiser, chief Cantor of Nyíregyháza in Hungary. Nyíregyháza is a city in north-east Hungary and the county capital of Szabolcs-Szatmár-Bereg.

Fülöp was a famous Cantor whose songs were recorded in 1908. Rumor had it that Fülöp's lineage dated back to a high ruler of the Khazars, and had converted to Judaism around 740 AD.

Alex was a big, heavy built man. He was almost six feet tall with wide shoulders and a dark complexion. He looked like a film star in a gangster movie of the 1940s. Alex had a great sense of humor and was very friendly, and never hesitated to assist when asked. It was easy to like him. The stories about Alex and his adventures were numerous, well-known to his family and to a small circle of close friends.

He had been a boxer in Paris during the carefree years of the 1930s.

He lived a very exciting life in France and traveled across Europe. A few years after he came back to Budapest from Paris, World War II erupted with the German invasion of Poland in 1939.

The Hungarians introduced forced labor in 1939, primarily aimed at the Jewish population. Jews were forced to serve in the Hungarian Second Army which fought the Russians. After the fall of Stalingrad in January 1943, the Hungarian Second Army was defeated. Most of the survivors were taken prisoner and sent to a Siberian labor camp.

When the Nazis entered Budapest in March 1944, Jews were forced to live in a ghetto, a well-guarded area around the synagogue.

They stayed there for only about three months until the Soviet army entered Budapest in January 1945, but meanwhile more than half the Jews had been sent to concentration camps.

Food was difficult to come by, so Alex crossed the border between Austria and Hungary several times, mainly carrying food for his family in the ghetto.

Life in Hungary was difficult during those days, especially for Jews, who were persecuted not only by the Nazis, but also by the local anti-Semitic Hungarians.

Alex, who couldn't accept the changes by his fellow Hungarians, became more and more involved with Zionist activities and had occasional political arguments with Arrow-Cross (Nyilas) members which ended with him using his boxing skills...

The Arrow-Cross was a national socialist pro-Nazi party.

They were active for a short period from October 1944 to March 1945, but during these six months they murdered over fifteen thousand Jews and were responsible for the deportation of over eighty thousand Jews to the Auschwitz death camp.

Alex was known to save many lives including those of his family.

The story goes that he eliminated an S.S. Nazi officer in one of the bars in Budapest, took his uniform and identity and removed his family and neighbors from the death train to Auschwitz towards the end of the war.

Along with many other languages, he spoke fluent German, so it was not difficult for him to be convincing.

When the Soviet army entered Hungary in January 1945, thousands of Hungarian ethnic Germans were arrested and transported to the Soviet Union as forced laborers. Many died there as a result of hardships and ill-treatment.

Alex had been captured during one of his border crossings and because he spoke German and was wearing a Hungarian uniform, he was sent to a labor camp in Siberia.

After several months he succeeded in escaping and returned to Budapest.

The year of 1944 was full of events, including the affairs of Rezső Kasztner's controversial rescue mission, and Raul Wallenberg and the train transports to Bergen Belsen.

During 1944, Kasztner met with Adolf Eichmann many times. Eichman was in charge of deporting the Hungarian Jews to Auschwitz in occupied Poland.

Another tragic event in 1944 was the famous story of Hannah Senesh (Szenes) or Szenes Anikó which took place in Hungary. She was dropped into Yugoslavia, together with other parachutists from Palestine in March 1944, just about a week before the Germans occupied Hungary.

Senesh crossed the border into Hungary, was captured, taken to Szombathely, put into prison and tortured. After five months in jail, she was convicted of treason and on November 7, 1944 was executed by a firing squad.

When Alex came back from Siberia in 1945 ("Demokratikus Hadseregel"), dressed in the Hungarian army uniform, he met Esther Hoch ("Hoch" means "high" in German and "Ram" in Hebrew), a widow with two small children.

She was introduced to him by his Mother, who had been hiding the Hoch family and other neighbors in their basement in the Budapest Ghetto during the war.

It was love at first sight and in a couple of months (October 21, 1945), she became Mrs. Esther Weiser.

Her family came from a small town on the border of Hungary and Czechoslovakia, Komárom.

The historical city of Komárom had been cut by the Czechoslovak-Hungarian border in 1920. The Czechoslovak part was called Komárno.

Komárom and Komárno were connected by a bridge and the two towns were used as a border crossing between Czechoslovakia and Hungary.

She was a Holocaust survivor from Auschwitz who had lost her husband, her eight sisters and two brothers and their children during the war.

She had survived with her two children Robert-Dov (born 1935) and Zsuzsi-Rachel (born 1937).

Esther was a beautiful woman with black hair and big blue eyes. She was only five foot four, but she had a great figure even after giving birth twice.

Her official education had ended after elementary school but continued in life experiences during and after the Holocaust.

She loved Alex and admired him for his courage and stamina.

"Wherever he goes, I'll follow him; whatever he does, I'll support him," she used to say.

Esther had been born on June 16, 1909 to Anna and Mor Schwartz in Komárom. Her father, Mor-Moshe Schwartz and her mother, Anna-Netti Wolf, both were born in 1871 in Komárom.

Her father died on September 4, 1941 and her mother on February 15, 1944. Anna's family had a goose farm and lived in Csorna, a small town in Győr-Moson-Sopron County, in Hungary.

Moshe's family was from Nagymagyar, a town in the district of Pozsony, province of Slovakia belonging to Hungary before the war and after the war to Czechoslovakia (The town's new name is Rastice).

His father was the *Shochet* (ritual slaughterer) of the town. Esther's first husband Erno-Zvi Hoch, a bank clerk, was murdered by the Nazis in 1944. He was 44 years old.

World War II ended in 1945 with the victory of the Allies. The USA and Soviet Union emerged as the main superpowers.

It was the beginning of the cold war that lasted for the next forty-six years. The UN was formed to replace the League of Nations, mainly to deal with nations' conflict and preventing war...

György-Moshe Weiser was born to Alex and Esther on March 22, 1947 in Budapest, Hungary. György or Gyuri, as he was called in Hungarian, is a typical name. In English or Italian he might be called George or Giorgio. The name exists in many other languages. It is of Greek origin and means "farmer."

On May 14, 1948, the State of Israel was established when the Jewish Agency proclaimed independence. It was the end of the British Mandate. Hungarian Jewry post-war post-Holocaust now had options, that is, to stay or to immigrate to Israel or elsewhere.

Zionists argued that now Jews must return to their original national roots, to their home land in Israel. However, the communists who gained power in Hungary in 1949 didn't accept this option.

It was a reactionary notion conflicting with their desire to create a socialistic society.

Accordingly, they closed many Jewish institutions and arrested Zionist activists. Zionism and mass immigration to Israel were not allowed. Jewish educational institutions were absorbed into the general national school system. Alex had worked in many areas during his youth. He was very skillful with his big hands, so he preferred manual jobs as they paid well. At the same time he was a merchant; he had good sense of arguing and negotiating for the right price.

Many years later the family told this story about his negotiating skills. Alex and his friend were at a chicken market and stopped next to a gypsy seller. They spent an hour while Alex was negotiating the price of a chicken until he reached less than half the asking price. When the gypsy became tired and finally agreed to sell, Alex just walked away. When asked why he didn't buy it, he replied, "I just wanted to see how low he would go..."

Just before the war, Alex had been trained and specialized in the design of leather upper parts of shoes.

Later he opened a workshop, which was quite successful. He used to say, "They can take away your wealth but not your skill," and "the more skills you have the more ways you can feed your family."

The Weiser's were active Zionists. Their big house in Budapest was often used for gathering of Jewish youngsters and as a last stop before leaving the country illegally.

With the encouragement of a representative of the Jewish Agency in Budapest and after long discussion and hesitation, they decided to immigrate illegally to Israel, using the opportunity of loose border checks and greedy guards.

3. The Capture at the Border Crossing.

THE BORDER CROSSING at Szombathely was usually manned with four soldiers. Two patrolled and two stayed at their post in small wooden barracks.

There was chief Miklos and his deputy Arpad, always inside playing cards, listening to music, and drinking and not always tea. They were stationed at the border crossing and lived nearby.

The two patrolling soldiers were young and inexperienced. They had weapons loaded with real ammunition but rarely if ever used these weapons. They were replaced from time to time with new recruits who had received new and conflicting instructions.

Before 1949 the instructions were to let immigrants pass, so their job was easy. They just sat there for many hours bored and doing nothing. However in early 1949, the communist government changed their policy.

They especially didn't allow immigration of Jews to Israel.

The guards were strictly instructed to stop everybody without proper documentation.

Those who were caught were imprisoned for a certain period and as punishment their property, including houses and other valuables were confiscated.

They also added prison time proportionally to the valuables they tried to smuggle out of the country.

At the border, the confiscated valuables were partly transferred to the authorities and partly divided among the guards...

Everybody knew that, including Alex. He had met with Chief Guard Miklos, earlier, who had been bribed accordingly to let the group pass.

Suddenly, all hell broke loose... strong lights were projected on the group accompanied by loud sirens.

"Everybody STOP!" cried one guard aiming his weapon, "Put your hands up" and "don't move or you'll be shot."

"This was not supposed to happen," Alex thought and was first to react.

He threw a small package of jewelry and buried it under the snow.

Lajos moved toward the guard waving his flashlight, starting to say:"…excuse me…" but he didn't finish his sentence; the bark of the guard's rifle stopped him…

"I said don't move" the guard shouted again with a shaking voice.

Alex cursed: "Az Anyád… did you have to shoot?"

The guard, a young soldier, who had rarely used his gun before, cried repeatedly, "I thought he had a gun… I thought he had a gun…"

Lajos was in pain, lying wounded on the ground. His wife Ilona cried franticly and fainted. Their son just stood there frozen with his hands up… reminiscent of similar awful sights during the Holocaust…

As it turned out, that night Chief Miklos had to leave his post early as his baby had become ill suddenly. His wife phoned, crying, and asked him to come home immediately to take them to the nearby hospital. He left instructions to his deputy, Arpad, who had forgotten to update the other patrolmen. Men, women and children were separated and put in jail. The children were taken to a Monastery for couple of months.

Alex was put in jail for six months and Esther for four months as she was pregnant. They received a minimum sentence. The rest were imprisoned between six and eighteen months as they carried valuable jewelry.

Esther's older children, Dov (age 14) and Rachel (age 12) had successfully crossed the border and reached Israel in the winter of 1949, a couple of days before the group's attempt to escape from Hungary. Gyuri (age 2), who was being carried by his father Alex, was put in a Monastery.

When the Weiser family returned to Budapest after release from prison, they discovered that all their property had been confiscated by the Hungarian authorities.

First, Esther was released from prison. She took Gyuri from the Monastery and went back to Budapest where she found a small apartment.

"It will do until Alex comes" she thought. Later he'll find a better place. When she tried to retrieve some of their possessions from the old house, she was not allowed in by the new tenants.

"Well, I'll wait. In less than two months Alex will be released and he knows what to do," she was thinking.

After about two months, at the train station late evening, Esther and Gyuri met Alex just released from prison.

He was angry, humiliated and went immediately to their confiscated house in Budapest.

"You stay here," he said to Esther, "I am not sure what is going on inside."

Esther saw him as he entered the house in order to get certain personal belongings.

Only after a loud argument with the new occupants of their house was he allowed removing certain personal belonging, but the big piano stayed there…

Alex put everything in a bed sheet with other stuff and put it all on a small wooden cart he had found somewhere. The apartment Esther found was a few blocks away from their previous house.

The cart was making noises as the wooden wheels knocked against the rough old paving stones.

Esther, who was almost eight months pregnant, walked heavily next to him while Gyuri was almost asleep, sitting on the edge of the cart.

In no time Alex found a better place in Kazinczy Street at the VII district in Budapest, walking distance from Rumbach and Dohany Street synagogues. He was a natural merchant-dealer. He left early morning and came back home late at night, sometimes only the next day. He was always very energetic, smiling and with self confidence.

He used to say to Esther: "You'll see my darling that the sun will shine upon you in Palestine."

He loved Esther and she adored him, Gyuri felt safe and happy.

Alex tried to keep in touch with the others from the night that they would never forget. Lajos Weisz recovered from his wounds, but he blamed Alex for everything. It was expected... The Rubinsteins went back to Debrecen. The Kleins lived near the Weisz family in Budapest. In spite of their proximity to the Weisers' house, they rarely met.

The Hungarian authorities were very harsh to those who tried to escape. Alex informed the group about a year later that he had filed an official request to immigrate to Israel and that he recommended that they do the same.

The first to apply were the Kleins, Agi, Mihaly and Pista, leaving Uncle Leo behind. It seemed that they were very eager to leave.

Later the Rubinsteins, Katy, Imre and Marika asked officially to leave the country but this time to the USA. They were told that it might be faster to get an immigration visa to the USA than to Israel and they were right. Ilona Weisz could not convince Lajos to apply. They got divorced and she applied for herself and for her two children, Michael and Eva. The Rubinsteins left for the USA in 1953, the Kleins and Ilona Weisz with her two children left Hungary for Israel in 1954.

Life in Hungary during those years was reasonable. In August 19, 1950, Tibor (Tibi)-Pinchas was born. Gyuri went to regular school in Budapest and also to the orthodox *Cheder* (meaning "room"), where he was taught religious education.

Unlike other Jewish families, who never encouraged their sons to use physical force Alex expected his son, his first born, to be strong and to be able to take care of himself. Gyuri was one of three Jewish kids in the regular school. They lived nearby and played together after school. Other children were constantly picking and cursing them: "Büdös Zsidó" "Stinky Jew."

In 1955, Gyuri celebrated his eighth birthday. On their way home from school, the three Jewish kids were stopped by three other kids. The other two Jewish kids were frightened and ran away leaving Gyuri alone behind. For Gyuri this was his first physical confrontation. He remembered his father's instructions: "Pick the strongest first, respond quickly, decisively and aim for his nose."

The nose was hit, but it was Gyuri's. The pain was strong and new for him. His eyes watered but surprisingly the glasses that he had been wearing since age six were still on.

The humiliation and the fact that he would have to face his father gave him the necessary courage and strength.

He hit back and hard. It was unheard of, a Jewish kid fighting... he felt his fist striking and knew that it would end there.

He walked home bleeding but with strange satisfaction. They never disturbed him again.

Needless to say, Alex was very proud of his eight year old son... "It is not important what injury you had, the question is what damage you have inflicted on your attackers," he said.

Only in March 1956, seven years after their escape attempt, were the Weisers allowed to leave Hungary and this time legally.

Alex never understood why the Kleins were the first to receive immigration visas to Israel. He was told that it was granted based on the time of application, but actually in this case, it was not done accordingly.

They were lucky to leave just before the October revolution, which started as a student demonstration against the Stalinist government of Hungary which had imposed unacceptable Soviet policies. Thousands were killed and injured. A loud whistle sound indicated that the train was about to leave Budapest central station.

Alex, Esther, Gyuri and his brother Tibi were on the train with their minimal allowed belonging and they were on their way to Palestine-Israel. For some reason, in the Hungarian language, during those days they didn't use the name Israel but "Palestina." It was the adopted generic name for the Jewish homeland prior to the establishment of the state of Israel and it remained for some time after Israel's independence in 1948 as well.

Slowly the train moved and Esther smiled and said: "Finally we are free"…

Alex was cautious, "Let's not celebrate until we cross the Austrian border. I don't trust them."

He checked the documents and the visa permits of all the family again.

It was a relatively a short trip to the border and the train slowed down.

"One last stop before freedom," Alex said hugging Esther.

The train stopped at the border, and two uniformed men boarded. One of them was probably a policeman and the other a customs officer; they asked for papers.

Alex handed them the documents with a nervous smile. They looked in a folder they had and again at the papers then they exchanged some words between them.

"Please come with us," one of them said.

"Are there any problems?" Alex startled.

"No, it is just technicality, but we have to check with our supervisor."

"I am not getting off the train and I won't leave my family here, so if you have any problem check it with your supervisor or bring him here. We have all the necessary documents," Alex said, raising his voice.

The supervisor came on board after a few minutes, breathing heavily. Alex recognized him instantly as it was Chief Miklos, the guard from Szombathely.

"So, here we meet again," Miklos said cynically.

"Yes and this time legally"…

"We'll see about that, come with me."

They left the cabin and stopped in the small space connecting two cabins. "Sorry about that, I had to play it for those two officers' ears, Miklos said nervously smiling.

"Are you going to make any trouble?" Miklos asked.

"I haven't done so for seven years; let's just forget it," said Alex.

Miklos knew that he was to blame for their capture at the Szombathely border.

Although they had spoken several times on the phone since then, he was still very nervous.

"Look, I could have killed you for what you did, but it is useless now; you owe me," Alex said. "Ah… I also know you found a few bags of jewelry."

"Listen," Miklos started to say, but he stopped when he saw Alex moving toward him.

"In spite of your denial, just let's leave it, I am going to have a new life, so good-bye and I hope we'll never meet again."

The family traveled through Austria and spent a nice week in Genoa, Italy before boarding the Shalom, the ship which took them to Palestine and Eretz Israel.

.

4. Life in the Promised Land.

THE WEISER FAMILY arrived at Haifa port, Israel in the heat of March 1956 and was greeted by Esther's two older children, nineteen year old Rachel and twenty-one year old Dov, dressed in his Israeli Navy officer uniform.

The reunion was unforgettable; everybody was crying. Registration at the immigration desk at the port was according to their Jewish names; While Esther remained Esther, Alex became Shlomo, Tibor was changed to Pinchas and Gyuri to Moshe. For some reason, they also wrote George, which was the name used later by the military.

From Haifa port they went straight to the Orthodox Chasidic quarter of Bnei-Brak called Wischnitz, a small neighborhood named after Wischnitza, a town in the Ukraine. They stayed there for about a year, mainly because of their uncle, Rabbi Davidovitz.

Moshe attended the religious orthodox school in Neve Achiezer in the Wischnitz quarter of Bnei-Brak.

It was a difficult time for the Rabbi... he complained to Shlomo that young Moshe was disturbing the peace by constantly asking questions. He was curious and couldn't accept the Rabbi's quoting from the Bible: "Naaseh V'Nishma", which means first we'll do and then we'll hear and understand or in plain English: "Just do what I tell you to do, explanation will follow"... Moshe wanted the explanation first...

On July 26 of that year, Egypt headed by Gamal Abdul Nasser decided to nationalize the Suez Canal. This act led to the Kadesh Campaign or the Sinai War, beginning on October, 29th 1956 and ending in March 1957. Moshe, who was almost ten years old, remembered the line of tanks and military forces passing by his house from north to the south and into Sinai. It was confusing scenery for the young immigrant, just arrived to live a new life in freedom.

The stay at this orthodox village was temporary and the Weiser family was happy to move to their permanent home in Ein-Hatchelet, a small immigrant village just established in the sand, north of Netanya.

Moshe attended the regular semi-secular elementary school until 1960.

He used to entertain his classmates when called to the blackboard by writing texts in Hebrew from right to left. He wrote by holding the chalk in his right hand and when he reached about the middle of the board he switched the chalk to his left hand and continued writing.

He was able to use both his hands with equal ability. However, his left hand was stronger than his right. In combat, the fighter may choose to face their opponent with either the left shoulder forward in a right-handed stance or the right shoulder forward in a left-handed stance; thus a degree of cross dominance is useful.

Some renowned ambidextrous persons were Einstein, Michelangelo, Leonardo da Vinci and Harry Truman. Some of the right brain qualities are imagination, risk taking, artistic abilities, philosophical thinking and creativity. Left brain people, on the other hand, are said to be practical, conformist, fast and systematic and have excellent comprehension skills.

Right brain people are considered to be subjective, and have wider perception and strong intuition, while left brain people are said to be more logical, rational and analytical.

Among the new immigrants settled in the new village of Ein-Hatchelet, there was a Hungarian speaking Rumanian family with two daughters, Lisa and Erika. Lisa was a beautiful fifteen years old, a graceful and mature ballet dancer. Years later she became Moshe's first love and lover.

In 1961 he started Bar-Ilan High School in Netanya. It was a religious school with a very positive reputation and well known teachers. Many of Moshe's friends joined him at this school, in spite of the fact that they all were not religious.

Moshe earned his first Lira (Pound) at the age of twelve, distributing political leaflets. As teenager, he worked at many jobs, such as orange picking, construction, laundry and deliveries, selling the fruits of Opuntia ficus-indica (Sabres) that he picked from a nearby field and tutoring, especially mathematics.

He earned enough so he was able to buy a bicycle and also a transistor radio, which was quite unique and expensive in those days.

Four years of study were not easy for Moshe. He had to overcome many personal and other difficulties.

In addition to the need to work after school, he was responsible for the large garden at home where he and Alex planted trees and a large variety of vegetables.

They also built a small chicken coop. It was like a mini-farm, part egg-producing chickens, housed in rows of battery cages, and part broilers for meat production.

Alex made a significant discrimination between his two sons.

While he pampered Pinchas and had no special expectations of him, his behavior toward Moshe was different.

He raised his first-born in a very strict manner, including occasional physical punishment as well.

Moshe was expected to be the successor, so he had to be like Alex, especially physically strong and tough.

Moshe received all the physical duties at home, repairing things, working and planting in the large garden, lifting, carrying things and taking care of their mini-chicken farm.

As the result, he developed muscles and stamina, and was capable to break bricks and other things with his bare hands. This skill helped him in later years in his Karate lessons.

In addition, he was the money-collector, visiting the many clients who owed them for goods and repair services. It was very common those days when most transactions were in cash and barter.

One of the clients who refused to pay his debt for a long time was visited by Moshe one evening.

When he returned with the payment, Alex was surprised and asked him how he did it.

Moshe told him that when the guy said that he would pay next week, he just sat down at the table and asked for dinner.

"I can't go home without the money; my Father will not let me in, so I'll stay here for the week until you'll pay..."

At their home in Ein-Hatchelet and at his brother Dov's place in Haifa, Moshe met with many of the Israeli navy officers including Yohai Ben-Nun, who was the commander of the navy from 1960 until 1966. He remembered occasions when his brother Dov came home with several of his friends from the navy and they stayed for the night.

Dov was the matchmaker who introduced his friend from the navy, Vili the "Gingi" (redhead in Hebrew) to his sister Rachel. Very shortly after their marriage Vili was injured in a commando exercise and was transferred after recovery to a desk job.

In later years the entire family was "married" to the navy, including Dov's son.

Atlit is a coastal town located south of Haifa, which was originally an outpost of the Crusaders.

The British authorities used to detain Jewish immigrants to Palestine in Atlit. Today there is a museum of the Ha'apala. A base of Israel's naval commando is located nearby. Atlit beach at the base was used by military personnel and their families during weekends.

Occasionally, Moshe joined his brother and his friends from the commando unit at that beach.

In 1966 he met with navy commanders there, such as Shlomo Arel, who took over the position of navy commander from Yohai Ben-Nun.

There Moshe also met with David Elazar (Dado) and his family when he was Chief of the Northern Command. Those meetings with such a high ranking and famous officers left a strong and unforgettable impression on young Moshe.

He finished his high school studies and was drafted into the Israeli army on the first of August, 1965.

Moshe continued to visit that beach whenever he had the opportunity.

5. Israel's Nuclear Capabilities.

IT IS WELL KNOWN THAT SHIMON PERES was one of the major forces behind the establishment of Israel's nuclear capabilities. In the late 50s almost everybody was against the plan.

"It is too expensive and too ambitious," they claimed. Even the military was against it, as they were afraid they would lose part of their budget.

After Peres raised the money from private resources, he had difficulties in recruiting the right people. One of his sources was young students from the Haifa Technion. However, existing scientific knowledge and other related technical information were insufficient to build the type of nuclear facility that was needed.

On the 6th of March 1963 a secret memorandum signed by Sherman Kent was sent to the special assistant to the President for National Security Affairs at the White House. Its title was: "Consequences of Israeli Acquisition of Nuclear Capability."

Sherman Kent was a history professor serving in the CIA since WWII. He had developed many original methods of intelligence analysis and was known as "the father of intelligence analysis."

He served as chief of the CIA Office of National Estimates (ONE) for fifteen years, under four Directors of Central Intelligence during four presidential administrations. The summary of that memorandum states that:

The most general consequence would be substantial damage to the U.S. and Western position in the Arab world. However much the U.S. expressed disapproval of Israel's achievement, it would be difficult to avoid an increased tendency for the political confrontation in the Middle East to take the form of the Bloc and the Arabs against Israel and its friends in the West.

Israeli "acquisition of a nuclear capability" may mean either:

(a) Israeli detonation of a nuclear device, with or without the possession of actual nuclear weapons, or

(b) An announcement by Israel that it possessed nuclear weapons even though it had not detonated a nuclear device.

It is not conceivable that Israel might manufacture a weapon according to acquired designs without testing through its access to nuclear technology in the international scientific community and possibly its special relationship with the French.

Kent in his detailed analysis memorandum predicts the outcome, the world response and particularly Arab reactions if Israel has nuclear capabilities:

The Arabs are united in their hatred of Israel, and would share a common fear of any Israeli nuclear capabilities. We do not believe, however, that they would prove able to act in any more unified or coordinated fashion than in the past.

Nasser might be tempted to strike at Dimona, but would probably be deterred by the fear that Israeli retaliation would destroy him before international peace-keeping machinery could intervene to suppress the conflict.

Nasser would contemplate, and might embark upon, a nuclear weapons program of his own, with what technical help he could beg or hire from abroad; but this would at least be a lengthy and expensive enterprise, highly provocative to Israel.

The principal advantage in the short term would be to give Nasser something to make speeches about. In his efforts to restore Arab morale, Nasser might claim to have non-nuclear weapons of mass destruction, chemical or biological, and might even make an effort to develop some capability along these lines.

The obvious recourse of the Arabs would be to turn to the Bloc for assistance or assurance against the new Israeli threat. We think it is virtually certain that Nasser and other Arab nationalists would take this course, yet it would be distasteful and unsatisfactory to them.

The Soviets would, however, see plenty of opportunity for winning political advantage.

According to their habit, they would seek to please the Arabs with resounding declarations of sympathy and support, and with dire threats against Israel or any other power that might dare to use military force against an Arab state. Experience from the time at the Suez affair suggests that these manifestations would indeed win friends and influence in the Arab world.

If the Israelis refrained from attacking the Arabs with major military force (as en believe they would), the Soviets might even persuade many Arabs that they had in fact been protected from destruction solely by the exercise of Soviet power.

In such fashion, without involving themselves in dangerous commitments, the Soviets would substantially enhance their influence and position throughout the Middle East, and perhaps find the basis for a firmer Bloc-Arab alignment against the West than they have so far been able to achieve.

6. The Secret Meeting at *The Room.*

IN THE SUMMER OF 1964 a meeting was held at a military location in Tel-Aviv.

The meeting took place at *The Room*, which was indeed a room in a highly guarded, but inconspicuous government facility. It was actually a room within a room, windowless and secure. A special access code was required to enter.

The room was furnished with a simple desk, a gray metal file cabinet with a lock, a sofa and four chairs. On the wall behind the desk was a large photo of Levi Eshkol, the Prime Minister next to a photo of David Ben-Gurion. There was a black telephone on the desk as well as some stationary items. The room was carpeted wall to wall with a rough gray carpet.

A heavy built, wide shouldered man was sitting at the desk. His name was Gadi but he was known as G. This was the naming system, never using the real name, not even the first name, only initials.

This led to certain problems-- how to differentiate two people with the same initials. It was solved simply on a case by case basis and an adjective was added, like red G. and just G. for the second guy.

Gadi was the new guy nominated recently by Levi Eshkol, the Prime Minister to assist in counter intelligence and act as liaison between various departments.

Normally, he worked near the Prime Minister's Office in Jerusalem and officially was known to be one of the many "consultants" to the Prime Minister.

In front of him there were two. On his left was Mike or M. He was tall and thin with glasses and grey hair. The third one was the youngest in the room, tanned, with blond hair, and blue eyes looking like a movie star. His name was Rafi or R.

"The instructions came directly from Eshkol," Gadi said.

"He accepted the plan brought to him with a few reservations. However, in general we do have a green light to proceed and we have to start looking for the right candidates."

"OK, so do we agree on the screening criteria?" asked Mike while leaning forward in his chair.

"Yes," Gadi answered shortly.

Rafi opened his mouth as if he was going to say something but he stopped when he saw Mike's reaction.

"OK, then to summarize, we are going to monitor new draftees and the initial criteria will be outstanding IQ, European or U.S. natives, English speaking or one of the European languages as mother tongue and they have to belong to *the right family*," Mike said.

"Sorry, but I still don't understand what you mean by 'the right family'... and why it is so important?" Rafi asked.

"Look, we have already discussed this, it is not going to be an "accept" or "reject" criterion, but it will be a screening factor if we have too many candidates.

We simply mean to dig a bit deeper as to the roots of the candidates, the values and loyalties to the country embedded in their family.

Obviously we'll check the immediate family and close relatives serving or having served in IDF or in other agencies," Gadi said, pausing while sipping from a glass of tea.

"We have enough suitable candidates for our regular positions within our planned budget. What we don't have are those "quiet people" with the almost perfect cover, difficult to connect to us or to any other government body. We'll be able to recruit such a person only if they are completely self-sufficient and independent. We need real people for very long periods, those who will integrate naturally into any location."

"You don't think that drafting at such an early age might not fit the plan and our long term expectations?" Mike asked.

"From your question... I think... you misunderstood the plan," Gadi said.

Let me tell you, he added, that if you think this is too early, there are rumors, that the Russians are recruiting entire families for the KGB.

They cultivate and train young teenagers especially for long term missions.

"We'll monitor their progress at the selected Universities or Institutions. They will develop a natural path to scientific and business related careers and only from that group will we actually recruit, but we'll start as early as possible," Gadi said.

"How will the info flow back?" Rafi asked.

"Pure business related meetings and scientific conferences will be the platform for receiving and transmitting info and instructions. Moreover, real business people will be the curriers.

The target is to generate the smallest cells as possible, which are most efficient and effective," Gadi said.

"Do our regular agents qualify for this mission?" Mike asked.

"No, we need a new type of agent for very long term work. They should have natural access to nuclear facilities and to related info. This will be a very compartmentalized operation.

We do have many requirements from those young recruits, in addition, and I reemphasize in addition to our regular requirements.

"How many will we have, eventually?" Rafi asked.

"My estimate is that from each round of new enlistees, we will screen potentially qualified recruits out of which hopefully we will find five. The target is to recruit about twenty people in the next five years.

We need unique individuals, where the initial parameter will be the IQ test we conduct normally; from that list we'll select those who are European or American born, speaking languages in addition to Hebrew and English, physically and mentally fit, and you know what I mean," Gadi said.

"So what is our current status and who is involved?" Mike asked.

"As I have indicated, the Prime Minister gave his OK to carry out the plan, which until now very few people knew about. The others will know only that we are recruiting for one of the organizations."

"What if...?" Rafi started to ask.

"Please, not now, let me finish. It is an unusual plan never tried before and you'll have plenty of time to ask later.

Now it is important that you listen carefully." Gadi said impatiently. "What we need is unique information in the nuclear area. Not standard knowledge, not only certain technical issues but much more than that.

We need to know ahead of time what others are doing in this area, I mean *all* others, now and what they plan to do in future. We have our regular agents in the field, but they have great difficulties accessing those facilities and they have been exposed quite quickly at several sites."

"Are there any more requirements?" Rafi asked.

"There are other requirements that I'll not mention now and we may change them on a case by case basis.

The idea is that we want to generate a new type of deeply covered highly intelligent agents, working long-term. They will grow and evolve with time, with minimal contacts and intervention."

Rafi couldn't resist Gadi's long monologue, "So what's new?" he asked, "How will those new recruits be different from the others?"

"They will not be our official employees, no direct traceable funding, no money line connection and minimal contact.

They will live in Europe or the U.S. with families and will have such an occupation that will require frequent worldwide travel," Gadi responded.

"Everything you have said and not in detail is leading to scientists. So why not recruit directly?" Mike asked.

"We are currently employing a few, but for this mission we need fresh unknown people, who will evolve to be what we need. They will be monitored for a couple of years before actually being activated."

"This is crazy! It's a ten year preparation and monitoring; where will they be in ten years, but more importantly where will we be?" Rafi cried.

"You don't get it... they will have assignments in less than five years; in seven and not ten years they will be in the field.

You have similar long term planning in establishing a football team as well," Gadi responded.

Moshe was drafted on 1st of August 1965 as George Weiser, first to armored forces.

In his basic training, he studied *Krav Maga*, Hebrew for "contact combat," a hand-to-hand combat system developed in Israel. Unlike most martial arts, *Krav Maga* is essentially a tactical defense skill. It is used by the Israel Defense Forces and a modified version was adopted by the Mossad, Shin-Bet, and also by the FBI and United States special operations.

"Well, I have over twelve candidates here. It is a good turn out for the graduating class of August 1965; they are usually considered to be the best recruits. Especially, I want to show you this guy who I believe is what we are looking for," Rafi said, in October 1965 during their scheduled meeting in *The Room*.

"What's so unusual about him?" Mike asked.

"His IQ is out of range..." was the reply.

"I took the liberty to check his family and they fit as well," Rafi said.

"OK, after basic training, you should assign him and the others to units with access to MAMRAM," commanded Gadi.

MAMRAM was a Center of Computing and Information Systems established in 1959 by the instructions of Brigadier Yitzhak Rabin, who was at that time the head of AGAM, the Department of Operations of the Israeli Defense Forces (IDF).

This unit was managed by a civilian computer expert, Mordechai Kikion.

After basic training, George was transferred to the Chief Supply Officer's headquarters, headed by Colonel Moshe Gat. He was stationed with a special unit of research with close operational relations with MAMRAM.

For the next two years, George served in various capacities as a "clerk" in the research unit and was exposed to top secret military information, including all field units, their locations, personnel, inventories and other sensitive military data.

7. The Six Day War Era.

ON JUNE THE 5TH, 1967, the Six Day War erupted between Israel and its neighbors. There was overwhelming Arab cooperation of Egypt, Jordan, and Syria. They were supported by additional troops and arms sent by Saudi Arabia, Iraq, Morocco, Sudan, Algeria and Tunisia. The result is known: Israel gained control of the Sinai Peninsula including the Gaza Strip, the West Bank, East Jerusalem, and the Golan Heights in the north.

Jerusalem was recaptured from Jordan on June 7, 1967 by the paratroopers of the Israeli Defense Forces.

It was a highly emotional moment for all Jews everywhere. For the first time in 2000 years Jerusalem's holiest site was under Jewish control.

All people involved in the liberation and reunification of Jerusalem, Lt. General Mordechai-Motta Gur, General Rabbi Shlomo Goren, Chief Chaplain of the IDF who sounded the Shofar at the Western Wall,

General Uzi Narkiss, Yitzhak Rabin, Moshe Dayan, Levi Eshkol and many others, will be remembered forever.

On June 9, 1967 George was on duty in Jerusalem. He felt the uniqueness of the historical moment, especially at the Western wall or the "Kotel" and its surroundings, the holiest site for Jews. A few days later, he visited certain sites in Sinai. Sinai had become an extended graveyard of Egyptian army equipment. The sight which is often remembered are the numerous shoes left behind by the Egyptian soldiers, who apparently ran better without them back towards Suez Canal area...

At one of the sites, George found scientific and other books in Russian, which indicated Russia's presence and training of the Egyptians. It is known in certain circles that during the Six-Day War, the Soviet Union planned to assist Egypt and Syria to overcome Israel. Those plans included among others, air support for ground operations and naval landing. However, due to the strong response of the U.S. in conjunction with disagreements among Soviet leaders, the plan was aborted.

In certain other circles, the situation was much more complex and dangerous. Shortly after the first signs that Israel was going to win the war, the White House received a message that Soviet Premier Alexei Kosygin was threatening a military action that might lead to a nuclear confrontation. This threat was backed by preparation for an air supported naval landing in Israel.

The Soviet intervention had actually been set in motion before it was aborted. Details of the operation were kept secret yet were known to Israeli intelligence, who reported in detail to the Americans.

The KGB's Foreign Intelligence Directorate had Israel as a target even before 1967. The direct involvement of Soviet personnel in Israel and Egypt was known.

Aharon Yariv of Israeli Military Intelligence reported to Eshkol that the Egyptians and Syrians acted as if they had the Russians' support.

Moreover, the Soviet Union was a contributing factor in escalating the Middle Eastern conflict to war.

Israeli Foreign Minister Abba Eban, who received the info from the Mossad, told U.S. Ambassador Barbour that the Russians were feeding the Egyptians and the Syrians with disinformation, especially about Israel's military positions and intentions.

The Russians were certain that Israel would be defeated and quickly.

This assessment, which was backed by the KGB, was the main supporting force behind the decision of those Arab states to join the war against Israel.

During his military service, George was exposed to computers and data processing, which later helped him to decide on his scientific career.

George was honorably discharged in October 1967, four months early, to enable him to start his studies at the Hebrew University of Jerusalem.

In reserve service, he was assigned to MAMCHI, the computer center of the Israeli Navy, where he received the rank of Res. Navy *Science Officer*.

"It has been four years since we started this program and we have only seven serious candidates. There are fewer than we expected; maybe we should update the requirements?" asked Mike in September 1968, while meeting in *The Room*.

"No, let's concentrate on those we have, and how is your favorite guy doing?" asked Gadi.

"He is doing very well," Mike said.

"His brother is also doing fine," added Rafi.

"Who is his brother?" Gadi asked.

"Actually, you might know him or have heard of him. You were an officer in the Navy Commando, weren't you?" asked Rafi. "He is Major; last year he attended PUM," Mike answered.

PUM is the Command and Staff College, the most elite instructional institution existing in the IDF system used by all three military branches, the navy, ground and air forces.

"He also received a special commendation from Rabin after the Six Day War. He was involved in a special operation executed by Shayetet 13," Mike reported.

Shayetet 13 is an elite Israel Defense Forces Naval Special Forces unit. The unit is considered one of the top three Special Forces units in Israel. They specialize in maritime hostage rescue and counter terrorist missions. Their missions have not been publicized except on rare occasions.

"Tell me about your guy; what was his name? George? How far did you go with the other training?" Gadi asked.

"He was at our facilities for a while. I wanted to see if in addition to his mental skills, he is physically fit as well." Rafi said and added, "About his name, he'll change it in the near future."

"OK and what was your conclusion?" Gadi asked.

"He took the advanced course in *Krav Maga* and did well... very well... there was an incident... the instructor asked him to perform a complicated exercise..." Rafi said quietly.

"And what happened?"

"The instructor was in cast for couple of weeks... it seems that he is one of our guys...

His geeky looks are quite deceiving... he can change his appearance and impression like Dr. Jekyll and Mr. Hyde," Rafi said.

"So we may use him also for tasks other than 'Science Officer'," Gadi stated with clear satisfaction.

"Yes indeed, he is a natural and will be a great asset to the unit," responded Rafi.

George arrived at the campus of the Hebrew University in October 1967 to start his studies for B.Sc. in Mathematics and Statistics. The program included supplementary studies of Economics and Computer Sciences.

On the 26th of November, Alex died at the Tel-Hashomer hospital, after suffering a long time from liver problems contracted in Siberia. He was only sixty years old.

At the funeral held in Holon cemetery, very few people attended-only the closest family, a few friends and neighbors.

However, the presence of two individuals, standing somewhat outside the circle of the other participants, was quite obvious.

"It's a loss to go so early," said one of them.

After Alex's death and with Esther's consent,

Moshe-George Weiser changed his name to Giora Ram in early 1968. Giora first met Menachem Begin in 1968 at a lecture at the student dormitory of Qiryat Yovel in Jerusalem.

A few years earlier, in 1965, Begin had headed the Gahal party, which was a union between Herut and the Liberal Party. In June 1967, Gahal joined a national unity government under Prime Minister Levi Eshkol.

It was a small room and there were less than twenty students gathered to listen to Begin's politics. He left a tremendous impact on everybody. He was a superb speaker who knew how to get his audience focused and enthusiastic. He spoke about many things; among others, he explained about ancient Israel and its fight against enemies. His speech was perfectly prepared and accompanied by facts and references; it was very impressive and convincing.

After the lecture, Giora asked him provocatively, if and when he thought he would be able to convey his messages in the Government with a real ministry position...

Begin was serving in the cabinet for the first time as a Minister without Portfolio. He looked at Giora, smiling and responded quickly, "My son, it will be sooner than many think"...

He was right... just a few years later, in June 1977, he became Israel's sixth Prime Minister.

Giora met Teddy Kollek several times at meetings in Jerusalem. Teddy Kollek was born in Nagyvázsony, 120 km from Budapest, Hungary and named Tivadar Kollek.

He was named Tivadar (which is Hungarian for Theodore) after Theodore Hertzl. He was a Haganah operative in the U.S. until 1952 and director-general of the prime minister's office under David Ben Gurion until 1963, but he will be remembered as the mayor of Jerusalem for twenty-eight years.

Teddy had been the contact person for the MI6 under the British Mandate over Palestine; he had provided information about right-wing Jewish underground groups and his code name was Scorpion.

The MI6 file on Scorpion was declassified after his death.

There were many discussions on the nuclear issue at many different levels in the Israeli government. One of them was held in *The Room*.

"It is important to pursue a vague policy about the question whether we have or do not have nuclear capabilities," said Gadi and added, "What is more important to achieve in this policy is the belief that we do have it."

"The question they will ask is whether we will use it," said Mike.

"They must think that if we are pushed to the corner that we will not hesitate to use it and moreover, that we have enough for all of them. As Samson said, "I'll die with the Philistines," replied Gadi dramatically.

"Let me tell you a story," Gadi said.

It's a folktale. There was a Chasidic man and his little son caught in the woods by a group of Cossack hooligans. They burned the Chassid and let the little boy live. Many years later, the boy became a big fat man. He was eating large quantities gluttonously.

One night at the local Rabbi's table, the Rabbi asked him why he ate so much; it is not healthy.

The reply was: "When the Cossacks come to burn me, I'll burn for hours and hours with large flame, unlike my father who burned in minutes because he was skinny..."

"I don't like this story," said Rafi.

"Then I'll quote from Robert Frost's poem: 'Two roads diverged in a yellow wood', or there are two roads to choose for the Arabs in a yellow desert..." said Gadi and added in a threatening voice, "All being said, it should send a clear message to all our current and future enemies. We want peace! We even are willing to go very far in concessions."

Rafi interrupted his monologue and said, "Unfortunately, they interpret our willingness to give-up territories as giving-in."

"Yes, you are correct" said Gadi, "However, if they decide to choose the other road, the road of war and terror, they must know that we are prepared for that as well."

"The problem is that they have a short memory.

They tried several times before, even with united forces and failed" said Mike and added, "Actually, time is working for us; with time we are becoming stronger and more determined. However what if they decide to use non-conventional weapons?"

Gadi responded aggressively, leaning forward and raising his voice, "The Arabs must know that in the worst scenario, we'll put on hell fire for thousands of years and make this bloody territory uninhabitable for generations and generations."

To finance his studies, Giora was employed at the Bureau of Statistics in the Prime Minister Office. He also worked with Archeology Professor Mazar in excavating Herod's floor in Jerusalem.

In the late sixties and early seventies, Professor Benjamin Mazar headed excavations of the Temple Mount area, which is believed to be the site of the first and the second Jewish temples. In addition, Giora sold flowers to tourists and taught private lessons in Mathematics. Giora received a special study grant from the Pinchas Sapir fund.

In his mathematical studies, in the area of Functional Analysis, he was exposed to Radon-Nikodym Theorem, which later was used for Computerized Axial Tomography (CAT) in medical imaging systems.

In his computer studies, the availability of facilities at the university was limited. Computer Sciences in the 1960s were linked to military applications.

The use of computers was essential and related to nuclear capabilities as well. It was very difficult, and complex to get a computer, even for regular research activities at universities.

Here is a quote from a top secret CIA document from the 17th of March 1969, declassified only on the 9th of September, 2005:

MEMORANDUM FOR: The Secretary of State Assistant to the President for National Security Affairs, Director, Central Intelligence Agency.

SUBJECT: Stopping the Introduction of Nuclear Weapons into the Middle East.

On February 27, 1969, I sent you a memorandum advising you I was persuaded that xxxxxxx at a rapid pace and may have both this year. I suggested that such developments were not in the United States' interests and should, if at all possible, be stopped.

Furthermore, I suggested we should meet at the earliest opportunity to consider measures which the United States could take to preclude further xxxxxxx.

Finally, I recommended we meet with the President, following our meeting, to discuss the difficult and dangerous issues posed by the possibility of nuclear weapons in the Middle East.

Since February 27 I have seen additional evidence of activity that would enhance xxxxxxx. I refer to the granting, last June and October, of export licenses for two CDC 6400 computers and one IBM 360/65 computer xxxxxxx.

As Dave Packard indicated in his March 14, 1969, memorandum the Secretary of State and the Secretary of Commerce, we believe the CDC 6400, in particular, could be a critical tool in xxxxxxx.

Although I understand one of the two CDC 6400s has been shipped, I strongly indorse Dave Packard's recommendation that shipment of the second CDC 6400 be withheld until we have had the opportunity to discuss this whole problem area.

I wish to repeat my request, moreover, that we meet at the earliest possible opportunity to exchange views on the possible introduction of nuclear weapons into the Middle East and that we maintain the closest possible consultation on all matters which could affect such an eventuality.

I would like to suggest a meeting in my office at 10:00 a.m., Saturday, March 22. If that time is not convenient, would you please suggest alternative times that would be preferable.

Giora was using both CDC 6400 as well as the IBM 360/65 for research work at the Hebrew University and later at the Weizmann Institute.

He received a B.Sc. in Mathematics and Statistics from the Hebrew University of Jerusalem, with supplemental studies in Economics and Computer Sciences in 1970.

8. Industrial Espionage.

INDUSTRIAL ESPIONAGE became almost a necessity for most modern countries. This type of espionage is sometimes referred to as mild or low-profile espionage activity.

However, it is often not less dangerous than other field operative activities. To get results, agencies usually have to invest in unique people for long periods of time.

This type of activity has to be played very carefully as an information leak from an organization may reveal the mere existence of a mole and terminate his or her activity permanently.

It is a very complicated and sophisticated long term espionage activity that requires diverse skills to get to the right position in the organization, access to the appropriate information and the ability transfer it.

There are many types, forms and ways to perform such espionage. Industrial espionage usually is referred to as economic or corporate espionage.

The main target is for commercial purposes. However, there are other targets such as those for national security purposes and this type of espionage is conducted by governments worldwide.

In such cases, the targets are corporations, mainly those based on sophisticated technology such as: aerospace, telecommunications, biotechnology and others.

Post war era industrial espionage has taken on additional forms such as sabotage. This act is performed in cases where the target is to cause delays in certain developments, such as industries developing advanced military weapons.

Recruiting agents has many forms. A good and simple way is to identify a dissatisfied employee who is willing to cooperate for financial benefits in conjunction with revenge.

An inside-job is considered one of the best ways to get the information needed.

In certain cases some convincing may be required to get the level of cooperation needed, which may include blackmail, bribes or benefits.

Although recruiting an insider is a favorable way, there is no comparison to the well-trained dedicated home agent. The use of inside agents or home agents may be at corporate level, government level or both.

In order to hide the original source ordering or requiring that data or process, there are often levels of operatives or organizations in between.

In certain cases governments prefer to do this type of spying rather than make use of their own intelligence agencies. Governments use their business delegates, students and academics for information gathering.

Industrial espionage during the period of 1960-1980 was very difficult. However, with the introduction of super fast computers and the Internet, it has become much easier to transfer data. Accordingly, new measures of counter-espionage have been developed, but they still have not eliminated the possibilities for copying and stealing information.

The U.S. National Counter Intelligence Center (NACIC), in their reports to Congress, has indicated the existence of foreign industrial espionage activities.

They reported that the main targeted industries are information systems, aeronautics, biotechnology, electronics, sensors, armaments, energy related materials, nuclear systems, telecommunications, space systems and weapons.

The methods of espionage include surveillance and specialized technical operations such as signal intelligence. The foreign students studying in the U.S. and foreign employees of U.S. firms and agencies are very common sources for recruitment.

There are similar activities during international conferences and trade fairs. Other sources are sponsorship of research projects in the U.S. and assigning foreign commercial or science officers to joint research and development projects. In addition, a vast range of disinformation is used in many areas. There is an extensive range of free or open information that can be and is exploited. There are many publicly accessed databases that are available to all. In addition, anyone can ask for information directly or via email, communicating with scientists and discussion groups.

Actually, these days it is almost impossible to hermetically close and protect information from leaking.

As long as data is kept digitally and online and humans or betraying humans are involved, guarding and saving information is very difficult.

According to the FBI, economic spying by countries considered friends or adversaries of the U.S. is increasing each year.

They have confirmed that hundreds of foreign counterintelligence investigations involving economic espionage are pending before the Bureau.

Such espionage can make an enormous contribution to the national security of the spying country.

The secrets of MIG-21, the drawing and structure of the French Mirage, nuclear components and technologies are some of the Israeli examples.

Not all so-called industrial espionage is really in that category. For example, in 1996 there was a U.S.-Israel conflict over an Israeli aircraft deal with China.

A document published by the Department of Defense and from the General Accounting Office (GAO) pointed towards Israeli espionage activities against the United States and Israeli thefts of U.S. military technology secrets, and confirmed that Israel had illegally retransferred U.S. technology from the largely U.S.-funded Lavi fighter program to China.

The U.S. Office of Naval Intelligence (ONI) claimed that Israel was retransferring sensitive U.S. military technology to China. They claimed that by the sale of Lavi fighters to China, Israel was violating U.S. law as that aircraft contained certain sensitive U.S. military technology that had the potential to threaten U.S. national security interests.

Very shortly after the publication of the document, the Pentagon cancelled it. Assistant Secretary of Defense for military intelligence, Emmett Paige, Jr. wrote that, "The content of the counterintelligence profile does not reflect the official position of the Department of Defense."

Certain Intelligence officials commented that such an act might downgrade the U.S.-

Israeli intelligence and security relationship.

The U.S. Congress was informed and was aware of those allegations, but no public action was taken by the U.S. government in response. The question is why?

If Israel had violated U.S. law and conducted vast industrial activities, why didn't U.S. government react and why? Not only was there no downgrading, but there was even an upgrading of the U.S.-Israeli intelligence and security relationship. The answer is quite complex. In many cases it looks like espionage, but it is not necessarily so... There are many layers of interests between U.S. and Israel, mostly mutual interests, including known and unknown counter-espionage activities. For obvious reasons, this phenomenon is not publicized. Cases in the past were quickly hushed by both governments. One of those cases was Yosef Amit in 1986. He was a major in Israeli military intelligence working in Unit 504, a top Israeli intelligence unit or a "small - Mossad", which was responsible for coordinating spies in certain Arab countries.

Amit disappeared in 1986. The claim was that Amit had been recruited by a CIA officer named Tom Waltz, who was based in the CIA's station in Tel Aviv.

There was very limited press in both countries and it was mutually and quickly hushed up.

There have been several cases where Israelis were accused of industrial espionage.

These involved sensitive technology used in manufacturing artillery gun tubes, design plans for a classified reconnaissance system, monitoring a D.O.D. telecommunications system to obtain classified information for Israeli intelligence, transferring advanced aerospace design technology to unauthorized scientists and researchers, avionics, missile telemetry and testing data and aircraft communications systems for intelligence operations, information on advanced materials and coatings, information regarding a chemical finish used on missile re-entry vehicles U.S.-Israeli espionage and counter-espionage activities are known to all parties involved.

When an Israeli official was asked about American spying on Israel, he responded saying, "Some things you don't hear about; you should ask the head of the CIA. He knows."

All countries are constantly engaged in espionage against each other, especially allies. However, such an activity would never harm U.S. interests if it were discovered.

In most cases, the U.S. doesn't need to spy on Israel as they get full cooperation in most areas freely from Israel, especially where the existence of mutual interests dictates such cooperation and the transfer of information or technologies.

The fact is that Israel is one of the richest countries in the world with regard to technologies and innovations.

Many U.S. top secret highly classified technologies were developed by Israelis. Technology transfer and retransfer move in both directions.

The Congress is aware of that as well. Some information in this context is known only on the appropriate level of "a need to know basis," both in the U.S. and the Israeli governments.

Giora decided to continue studying Computer Sciences. He had two options, one of them was at Stony Brook University in New York and the other was at the Weizmann Institute in Rehovot in Israel.

Stony Brook had a large campus on Long Island's North Shore, with a world famous computer science department, especially in the area of Artificial Intelligence and Pattern Recognition.

After considering both options and advice from certain sources, Giora started at the Weizmann Institute in September 1970.

At the Institute he was engaged in various scientific activities including being a research assistant in the Geophysical Laboratory of Prof. A. Ben-Menahem and Dr. H. Jarosch, developing and implementing computer algorithms and programs to process and analyze seismology and physics related data.

One of those programs was related to Radon-Nikodym, the basis for the CAT scan invention lead by Godfrey Hounsfield and Allan Mc Cormack from EMI, England. They received the Nobel Prize for their work in 1979.

Giora also developed computer programs at the Weizmann Institute working on Digital Equipment Corporation (DEC) PDP 11&15.

He programmed compilers and interpreters for FORTRAN, BASIC, LISP and SNOBOL computer languages some time before Bill Gates made his deal with IBM.

On December 1971 the meeting was held in a new *Room*, in a conspicuous high-tech building in Tel-Aviv area. A special setup for this operation had been created and it was called *Ha-Yechida* in Hebrew, which means "The Unit." They occupied a complete floor at the top of the building. It looked like a regular high-tech company. The sign on the door read: "Imaging Exploration Company.

Two secretaries were receiving visitors at the reception desk. The reception area was quite large and the appearance was of a wealthy high-tech or law office. Behind the reception desk, there was a door requiring a special card to enter. When you passed through that door you faced a round corridor with offices around it. The *Room* was in the middle and required another security card to enter.

"Well, it seems you were right about Giora," Gadi said.

"He finished his studies at the Hebrew University and received his degree in mathematics and statistics and was accepted at the prestigious program at the Weizmann Institute where he will study Computer Sciences," Mike reported.

"Yes, I'm aware of that, but what is exciting is that he is at the Geophysical Laboratory.

I'll not go into details now about what it means for us, but I am happy with his progress," Gadi said with some satisfaction.

"What can you tell us about Giora, Mike?" Gadi asked.

"Well, I am not sure if you remember, but he was serious when he said that the two things he would never do were commit suicide or treason." said Mike.

"When was that?" asked Gadi.

"During discussions about if and when he was caught..." Mike leaned back.

He was annoyed at being interrupted and he continued his report.

"Giora's visual memory capabilities are outstanding, in addition to his ability to notice small details. For example, he can walk into a restaurant and after being there only a few minutes, he can tell the exact layout, the people, colors, suspicious characters, food types and many other minor details," Mike reported.

"What about his personality?" Gadi asked.

"Giora has a very complex personality and it was quite difficult to read him. At first he seemed to be very friendly, talkative and open."

"Do you mean... he has a big mouth?" asked Gadi, worrying.

"After being with him a while, you may discover that you know very little about him and you voluntarily gave him all info he asked," said Mike and added, "The biggest compliment he received from a fellow co-worker is that you talked for hours and said nothing valuable to me."

"So, yes... Big mouth says nothing..."

"OK, so you mean exactly what we need..." said Gadi, relaxed.

Sometime after Alex's funeral, Giora was summoned to meet Gadi.

"You wanted to see me sir?" asked Giora.

"I guess you don't remember me; it was many years ago," said Gadi, smoking his pipe. I was at Alex's funeral in 1960, where I met you and your family.

"Sorry but I don't have that memory," said Giora. "I understand you knew my Father."

"Yes, your father was known to us; I met him several times. He was a great man, and I always admired his courage and persistence. He was a true Zionist and we all miss him."

"Thank you sir, I miss him as well, especially when I need advice to choose between emotional and logical decisions or actions," said Giora.

"Well son... you can always come to me," said Gadi warmly.

"Thank you sir."

9. Nuclear and Satellite Technologies.

TESTING OF NUCLEAR BOMBS was and still is conducted deep underground at remote locations. Sometimes it is done deep under the sea. These actions are closely monitored by the regulatory bodies and by other nations.

The U.N. general Assembly adopted a Comprehensive Test Ban Treaty (CTBT) which was signed by over 145 countries. The Limited Test Ban Treaty (LTBT), which was signed in 1963, prohibits nuclear tests in the atmosphere, space and underwater. However, it did not prohibit underground testing. To monitor violations, networks of sensors were installed around the world.

The U.S. national data center for the CTBT is operated by the Air Force Technical Applications Center (AFTAC). AFTAC was assigned to monitor nuclear explosions in 1949, when the U.S.S.R. detonated their first nuclear explosion, and set up a secret network of seismic and other sensors worldwide; this is the Atomic Energy Detection System (AEDS).

The U.S. and other countries utilize technical means, such as satellite imagery, sensors on satellites to detect nuclear explosions in the atmosphere and space, and other intelligence methods.

The *British New Scientist* reported on October 12, 1978 that geophysicists in Germany and England believe that the earthquake in Tabas, Iran, in which at least twenty-five thousand people were killed, may have been triggered by an underground nuclear explosion. It might be that the Iranians had certain problems that were responsible for the disaster.

A seismic laboratory in Uppsala, Sweden, recorded a Soviet nuclear test of unusual size, maybe over 10 megatons at Semipalitinsk, which occurred only thirty-six hours before the earthquake.

At the geophysical lab of the Weizmann Institute between 1970 and 1973, Giora was involved in filtering seismic signals, separating the signals of real earthquakes and the signals generated by explosions. It was an essential step for validating and evaluating the occurrence and the magnitude of an explosion.

In addition to his many activities at the Institute, Giora was also in charge of student entertainment. Actually, he was a kind of a DJ.

He organized dancing evenings, inviting girls from the local nursing school of the Kaplan medical center and from the Faculty of Agriculture of the Hebrew University located nearby in Rehovot.

Meyer Weisgal was Chaim Weizmann's aide and chairman of the Executive Committee of the Weizmann Institute from 1949 until 1966 when he became president of the Weizmann Institute until 1970. Weisgal was an entrepreneur, not a scientist; however he had the understanding and the sensitivity of the scientific spirit.

The existence of British espionage in Israel during the 50s was common knowledge; the British became more active in 1959 when they realized that things were happening when Shimon Peres was given the role of Deputy Defense Minister.

The British Embassador invited Weisgal for a dinner and he learned from him that Peres was the driving force to get the Bomb.

Giora met Weisgal at the Institute when he published his autobiography in 1972 entitled *So Far*. Meyer gave Giora a copy of his book with 32 black and white historical pictures, signed it and said with a smile, "Promise me that you'll read it."

"We need satellite related information," Gadi said during one of the meetings held in early 1973. We have the general data. What we need is inside detailed information from an actual satellite project."

"I know exactly what you mean, and I think I may have a quick solution to this problem," responded Mike.

The European Space Research Organization (ESRO) was founded in 1964 by ten European nations for the purpose of space research. ESRO was based on the Conseil Européen pour la Recherche Nucléaire (CERN), which was an international scientific nuclear research institution.

The European Space Agency (ESA), which replaced ESRO, entered into the areas of earth observation, telecommunications and other space related applications and activities.

While ESRO was searching for the expert they needed for their satellite program, they found Giora at the Weizmann Institute in Israel. In order to avoid political and other bureaucratic problems, as Israel was not member in ESRO, Giora was introduced via a Danish firm located in Herlev, Denmark, working for ESRO as subcontractor. In early 1973, Giora made a few visits to Europe, meeting with several companies that were involved as subcontractors to the space research center in Germany. He presented his special skills and scientific abilities in conjunction with appropriate references.

When he returned to Israel he was confident that he would have to relocate to Germany. He was excited because of the challenge and the mission, but not so about the location.

He received his Masters (M.Sc.) degree in Computer Sciences with a focus on Image Processing from the Weizmann Institute of Rehovot. At a party organized by a friend, Giora met an active and a very smart young Hungarian speaking woman.

On August 21, 1973, she became his wife. The wedding, held at the Weizmann Institute, was unique. Prof. Israel Dostrovsky, the Institute President, attended the wedding.

Giora was very proud to see him among his many friends and relatives. Prof. Israel Dostrovsky was a nuclear chemist in the field of isotope research, and director general of Israel Atomic Energy Commission (IAEC) when Levi Eshkol was Prime Minister.

In September, immediately after his wedding, ESRO chose Giora, from among a large number of international candidates, to develop their METEOSAT satellite image simulator in Darmstadt, Germany.

The primary goal of the METEOSAT weather satellites was to provide visible and infra-red day and night cloud cover data and distribute the processed image data to certain users. METEOSAT-1 was successfully launched on the 23rd of November 1977 at Cape Canaveral.

The newlyweds left Israel in September 1973 to join ESRO in Darmstadt Germany. They rented a small apartment in Weiterstadt, which is a small town in the Darmstadt-

Dieburg district in Hesse, about six kilometers northwest of Darmstadt.

Shortly after they settled down, on October 6, 1973 Israel was attacked by a coalition of Arab states supporting Egypt and Syria; it was the Yom Kippur War.

Giora contacted Israel via its embassy in Berlin and left a message that he was willing to return immediately. The negative reply was swift and short, "Stay!"

The work at ESRO was challenging. Giora was given the complex task of sophisticated program development, which was comprised of many modules and modalities in the area of satellite image processing and simulations.

Giora attended The International Federation for Information Processing (IFIP) Congress that was held in Stockholm, Sweden in August 1974.

He made many interesting and useful contacts at this Congress in addition to having the opportunity of meeting Carl Gustaf (XVI), King of Sweden. He was also working with the European Space Technology Center (ESTEC) at Noordwijk, The Netherlands.

ESTEC engineers were responsible for the integration of scientific instruments to be loaded onto the satellites and to test functionality of all their payloads.

They were responsible for making all the arrangements and preparations for successful and functional launches.

Giora assisted the Dutch satellite program in resolving certain technical problems. They were very happy with Giora's performance at ESRO, so they offered him various possibilities to stay. Particularly challenging was the Spacelab project.

Back in August 1973, the American National Aeronautics and Space Administration (NASA) and ESRO agreed to join forces on a joint project to build a laboratory to be used on space shuttle flights. The actual construction of the Spacelab started in 1974 and they needed Giora's skills.

In early 1975, Haia, Giora's wife became pregnant with their first child and they wanted to have the baby in Israel. She was reluctant to go back to live in Germany and Giora felt that it might be a good time for a change.

After serious consultations, they decided to go home, back to Israel.

During those two years with ESRO, Giora accumulated extensive experience specifically related to Satellite data processing which he brought with him when he returned to Israel.

According to the foreign Press, the Israeli Air Force has three squadrons equipped with Jericho nuclear-tipped missiles.

They are located at the Sdot Micha base, 45 km south of Tel-Aviv. The Sdot Micha Jericho base is located near the town of Beit Zachariah, east of Ashkelon, south east of Tel Nof and south of the Sorek River. It is reported that classified satellite imagery reveals over 200 missile emplacements.

They have both Jericho I and Jericho II missiles. The Jericho-I missile was developed in the late 1960s with a range of over 500 kilometers. The Jericho-II is an advanced version with a range of well over 1,500 kilometers. However, the new Jericho-III nuclear missiles are based on Shavit space launch vehicles with a range of up to 7,000 kilometers.

The underground bunkers in the Judean hills house over one hundred nuclear Jericho missiles. The Israelis have a plan for the "second wave" with delivery using those Jericho missiles.

Air delivery of nuclear warheads could be made by the F-4E, which is a low level flying, two-seat, twin-engine, multiple role tactical Phantom fighter-bomber, the F-15, the Eagle, which is an all-weather, highly maneuverable, tactical fighter, the F-16, the fighting Falcon, which is a multi-role jet fighter aircraft originally developed by General Dynamics for the United States Air Force or by *other* aircraft.

The delivery systems include intercontinental ballistic missiles. Some are installed in Dolphin submarines acquired from Germany and modified by the navy. They are equipped among others with harpoon cruise missiles with nuclear capabilities and range of about 2,500 Kilometers. Early in 2002 Ikonos imagery showed that the facilities of Israel's Jericho missile base probably support storage facilities and may serve as a central ammunition depot for Israel.

Ikonos is a commercial earth observation satellite able to collect high-resolution imagery.

This view is supported by declassified Corona satellite imagery. The Corona program was a series of U.S. reconnaissance satellites developed and used by the CIA Directorate of Science & Technology with cooperation and support of the U.S. Air Force. According to Intelligence reports and asserts, Israel has a diversified range of toxic substances, nerve-paralyzing and incapacitating substances in the area of chemical and biological weapons.

It should be noted that the information of Israel's nuclear arsenal and locations of related and other military activities, are well documented and in part referenced by diverse publications that are available from the Internet and from declassified top secret documents released to the public by the CIA and by the British MI6. The number of nuclear weapons Israel may have is not so important when you have such a diversified range of different types and sizes, especially when the number is over five hundred…

In mid-1975, the Rams returned to Israel and Giora joined Elscint Ltd. to develop the first Nuclear Medicine data processor and analysis system (DYCOM).

Giora was sent to Elscint's London based International Sales and Service office in 1978 as Product Manager.

In London he was accepted by the British Council for National Academic Awards (CNAA) for Ph.D. studies in Medical Physics and Imaging at the Royal Postgraduate Medical School and Hammersmith hospital.

His Ph.D. work was finished, published and submitted two years after he started his studies. The work entitled "The Application of Image Analysis Techniques in Diverse Scientific Fields" was filed with the British Library and his research was published in various international scientific journals.

Certain academic regulations required a minimum study period, so his Doctorate was officially awarded in London only in 1984.

10. Unique Worldwide Adventures.

It is common knowledge that South Africa was able to mine uranium ore locally for use in the development of weapons since the late 70s.

The Kalahari Desert was the test site selected by The South African Atomic Energy Board (AEB). The plans were for tests to be performed about 250-300 meters underground. The high-security weapons research and development facilities were common knowledge.

Soviet intelligence detected test preparations and U.S. intelligence confirmed the existence of the test site. The Soviet and Western governments were convinced that South Africa was preparing for a full-scale nuclear test.

A U.S. satellite (Vela) detected on September, 22 1979 an unusual double flash over the Indian Ocean. It was assumed to be an Israeli - South African nuclear test. It was labeled as the "Vela Incident."

A former Soviet spy, Commodore Dieter Gerhardt, who was the commander of South Africa's Simon's Town naval base, said,

"Although I was not directly involved in planning or carrying out the operation, I learned unofficially that the flash over the Indian Ocean was produced by an Israeli-South African test." This operation was code named "Phoenix."

Later, he claimed that Israel had agreed in 1974 to arm eight Jericho II missiles with special warheads for South Africa. It was common knowledge that South African projects to develop nuclear weapons during the 1970s and the 80s were carried out with some cooperation from Israel.

In 1977 Israel supplied about 30 grams of tritium in exchange for fifty tons of uranium. Tritium is a radioactive isotope of hydrogen, used among other things, to boost a fission bomb. Israel also assisted in the development of the RSA-3 ballistic missile.

It was also suspected that South Africa signed a unique agreement with Israel that included the transfer of military technology and the manufacture of at least six nuclear bombs.

The abovementioned is substantiated by a secret CIA document from the 8th of June 1981.

The list of weapons of Israeli origin in the South African arsenal is extensive, a testimony to past large-scale arms trade between the two sides. Included in Pretoria's inventory are Reshef-class patrol boats, Gabriel surface-to-surface missiles, Gallil rifles, and Uzi submachine guns.

Speculation about South African-Israeli collaboration in producing nuclear weapons has been rife since 1963, when Pretoria sold Tel Aviv 10 tons of nominally safeguarded uranium.

Prime Minister Vorster's proposal in 1976 for a series of scientific and technical exchanges and the reports linking South Africa and Israel to the September 1979 "event" in the South Atlantic have raised speculations to new heights.

No similar exchanges have taken place between the Israeli Atomic Energy Commission and the South African Atomic Energy Board, and both the Israeli reactor complex at Dimona and the South African uranium enrichment plant has been closed to foreigners.

Although there is room for continued growth in South African-Israeli relations, the phase of rapid expansion may already have run its course. The outcome of the election this month in Israel could have a dampening effect.

Prime Minister Begin's primary challengers in the Labor Party have over the years made clear their reservations about bilateral ties and under a Labor government Tel Aviv could be expected to put some distance between itself and Pretoria. Some cooling in relations could occur even if the Likud bloc stays in power.

Yehia or Yahya El-Mashad was born in Egypt in Benha on January 1, 1932.

He attended school in Tanta, Egypt's 5th largest city, located about sixty miles north of Cairo and about eighty miles southeast of Alexandria.

In 1952 he graduated from the Department of Electrical Engineering at Alexandria University.

In 1956 he received his doctorate in Physics from London University.

Later he spent six years in Moscow, specializing in of nuclear reactor engineering. Upon his return to Egypt in 1963, he joined the Egyptian Association of Nuclear Energy and was a Professor of Engineering at the University of Alexandria.

While attending the first European Nuclear Conference (ENC-1), organized in Paris in 1975, he was recruited by the Iraqis. It was the same year when the Iraqi nuclear program was launched.

Yehia liked women and antiques. He spent many hours browsing in Parisian antique markets searching for collectables. He also was involved in seeking out certain types of women and he found them in Paris. There he met with Marie-Claude Magal. Marie was beautiful, tall and well built and she was submissive in the way Yehia liked.

It is known that enriched uranium can be used both as a fuel in nuclear power stations and as a component of nuclear weapons. The first supply of uranium was received by Yehia in Baghdad. The quality was not according to the required specifications and he flew to Paris.

When he was asked why he had to go himself for a task that one of the junior engineers might perform, he stated that he wanted to make sure that future shipments would comply with the specifications. Actually he wanted to be with Marie.

Clignancourt market or as it is known, Marché aux Puces St-Ouen de Clignancourt, on the northern edge of Paris, is the biggest flea market in the world. It has about 1,500 shops and stalls.

At one of the stalls, a visitor was examining a Damascene silver inlaid jar.

"A unique item isn't it?" commented another visitor.

"It is nice, but they are asking too much for it," was the response.

"Yes, but it is still a cheap price to pay, especially if you want to live long enough to enjoy it." It was the first time Yehia had been warned about his nuclear activity.

Yehia was startled. "Who are you?" he asked. "I am not important. It is just a friendly warning from your neighbor. Go home and be a Professor."

The second warning came on August 13, 1979 at a conference in Berlin. It was the International Conference on Structural Mechanics in Reactor Technology.

At lunch time, Yehia was carefully selecting his meal and asked about the type of meat on the menu.

"Is it beef or pork?" he asked. It took a while for the waiter to respond in mixed German and English.

"Nein zis iz no schwein, zis iz cow, mu mu…" and the man sitting next to him said, "You worry not to eat pork and you worry about the safety of the reactor you are about to build, but what about your safety and the future of your family? This is the second and final warning."

On June 13th 1980, on Friday evening, Dr. El-Mashad was found dead in his room in the Hotel Meridian in Paris.

His skull had been smashed (not as claimed that his throat was slashed).

A few days later Marie died in a car accident in Saint-Germain Boulevard.

As Product Manager traveling between hospitals and scientific institutions worldwide, Giora accumulated extensive marketing and technical information, which he passed back to his employer.

Among the proposals were the specifications and the need to develop a dual-head Gamma camera and Positron Emission Tomography (PET).

At the Royal Marsden Hospital in London, Giora developed and implemented a PET computer program using a Gamma camera. As his novel proposals were somewhat premature, they were rejected by the company.

The two years with Elscint based in London was very exciting and a highly active period for Giora. He traveled extensively all over the world, but mainly throughout Europe. He knew each border crossing, official and unofficial. From time to time he carried certain sensitive materials. In one occasion, he was almost caught by a zealous custom officer at Milan airport. The Italian Israeli intelligence relationship goes back to Benito Mussolini's fascist Italy period.

Before the establishment of the State of Israel, the Italians assisted in immigration and in weapon supplies.

One example of such cooperation was in 1948, when Fiorenzo Capriatti, a fascist who was close to Mussolini, came to Israel and trained the young Israeli navy commando unit, Shayetet 13. Since the establishment of the State of Israel, there has been close cooperation between Italy's intelligence service (SISMI), and the Mossad. It is known that Italy's intelligence services are one of the friendliest in the world toward their Israeli counterparts.

Milan's Malpensa International Airport is situated forty-five kilometers northwest of Milan. Giora was carrying with him two large round disks of Data General Computers. The disks contained two 14" double-sided platters, one fixed and one removable.

"Open it," asked the custom officer.

Giora took one of the disks and opened it. The officer, who probably had never seen such technology tried to put his finger inside, but Giora pulled it away and said in Italian,

"Attenzione! Medicina Nucleare."

The custom officer became pale and called loudly to his colleagues for help. They closed the area around Giora. It took a while to explain that they could not open it as it might destroy the important program material which was to be delivered to one of the local hospitals... Giora deliberately drew their attention to one of the disks. The second one looked the same, but it wasn't. After successful release from customs, Giora went on his way to a meeting in Bari.

He knew that it was much better to enter a country via its large international airport rather than arriving at a local small airport. The probability of getting caught with sensitive material when you are among hundreds of passengers is much less than arriving with few people when most of them are locals.

He rented a small Fiat and drove from Milan via Bologna, made a short stop at Rimini, continued to Ancona, and then down to Bari. The roads along the Adriatic seashore were gorgeous and he enjoyed the scenery very much. The meeting in Bari was held at the department of Nuclear Medicine in the La Madonna hospital.

He had held many similar meetings throughout Europe, usually at the Nuclear Medicine departments of certain hospitals requiring his expertise and involvement.

Giora gave his training lecture in a small room with about a dozen participants, mainly the local staff. He was searching for his contact but she found him. There was an immediate click between them.

She was working at the hospital as the Gamma camera operator in the Nuclear Medicine department. She spoke with a musical accent and Giora recognized it immediately. It was Hungarian. Her family had fled Hungary in November 1956, when she was only two years old. There was no need to change her first name Franciska, which is a Hungarian form of Francesca, meaning *free*. She was young, tall and redheaded with high energy. She was very perceptive. The meeting in Bari was very productive.

The Monte Carlo Casino is one of the most notable tourist attractions of Monaco, especially after Ian Fleming's first James Bond novel, *Casino Royale*.

Giora met with Rainier III, Prince of Monaco and his daughter, Princess Caroline at the Casino in Monte Carlo. It was during a medical conference reception in 1979.

After the reception he couldn't resist and went straight to the roulette table.

As a mathematician he knew the odds and at the same time he was quite aware of the entertainment factor as well. He decided to make it quick and put $ 500 on the red with a primitive assumption.

"If I lose I'll go to sleep early; however if I win I'll play with their money…"

He spent almost all night in the Casino. At first he had a strike of wining of couple of thousand dollars, which drew the attention of certain ladies in the room.

Eventually, he went to sleep with a small win but with a big smile.

Giora left Elscint in London in 1980 and joined Capintec Inc. in New Jersey, USA as Director of Research and Development.

It was considered a promotion and engaging in new area always was exciting.

Capintec has been recognized in the previous four decades as a world leader in the development, manufacturing and marketing of radiation measuring and monitoring instrumentation.

They had products with many medical and other applications mainly in Nuclear Medicine, Nuclear Cardiology, Radiology, and Radiation Therapy Planning.

As such, Capintec had natural access, via suppliers and subcontractors, to certain components which were essential components for nuclear related applications.

At Capintec, Giora was responsible for the development a multi-modality imaging system (PACS) which was presented at the Radiological Society of North America – the RSNA meeting in Chicago in 1982. He was also involved in the development of a Radiation Therapy Planning (RTP) system. In winter of 1982 Giora decided to end his stay in the U.S. and planned his return to Israel. Based on his extensive knowledge and experience in the field of imaging, he began looking for investors and partners for his project.

Giora met with Kobi Alexander, Boaz Misholi and Yechiam Yemini at Dr. Yemini's office at Columbia University in New York.

Giora was presented with their fresh business plan, seeking funds for their newly formed telecommunication company named Efrat.

Unfortunately, they couldn't find mutual interests in establishing a certain joint venture in the Digital Signal Processing area.

In later years they renamed the company Comverse Technology and became very successful after going public in the NASDAQ.

11. Scientific and Business Activities.

IN EARLY 1983 Giora returned to Israel to start his private business activities as a consultant. One of his first projects was the establishment of the Imaging Laboratory at Tadiran Ltd, where he carried out imaging related activities that were part of the new Israeli aircraft project – the Lavi.

It was a most stimulating project where Giora could combine his skills and experience in Digital Image Processing together with military specifications. The project was canceled by the government after a short period, but the technologies developed survived to be applied elsewhere.

In the summer of 1983, Giora had received a call from a friend in the U.S. asking him to consult a group of American entrepreneurs who were interested in buying an Israel medical monitoring company in Haifa.

He prepared a report which clearly indicated that the company was in fact in bankruptcy status.

The technology was obsolete, the eighty seven employees were not really working and the attorney who ran the company had no idea about medical technologies.

In order not to be so negative, Giora proposed a reorganization plan with new related technology in patient monitoring areas which would require a significant cash injection to implement the proposed plan.

In spite of the report, they bought the company.

Giora was puzzled and surprised, but the bigger surprise was when they asked him to implement his plan and offered him a free hand as President of the company.

It was a strange deal. They bought the company for one dollar assuming all the company's liabilities.

The first financing came from a Scottish conglomerate who actually owned the company.

The rumor was that the Scotts were laundering a certain slush-fund generated from their Hungarian activities, during WWII.

Dr. Khaled Abu Yusuf was a Medical doctor and a terrorist. He ignored his Hippocratic Oath when he joined a little-known cell of a radical Muslim terror group mainly active in Europe.

He was born in Lebanon to a wealthy family, but studied and lived in Italy.

He specialized in Nuclear Medicine and worked in Modena.

It was during one of his trips to visit his family in Lebanon that he was recruited and trained by Hezbollah. Dr. Khaled was very effective in marking targets and assisting in various terror activities during the 80s.

One of the targets was the Synagogue in Modena. The Synagogue is located near the Palazzo Comunale, which was built in 1873.

For some reason this target was abandoned, probably because they found another or maybe they didn't want to generate unnecessary conflicts with the Italian government.

Dr. Khaled loved the good life and was an amateur skier. He attended a medical conference at Marilleva ski resort in Italy. It was the 7th International Congress on Cardiology held during the week of January 27, 1986.

He died in a skiing accident at the ski resort on January 28, 1986.

It was the same day of the space shuttle Challenger disaster. It seemed he took a wrong turn where the track was for professional skiers and he fell to his death.

As President, Giora implemented a new and a comprehensive reorganization plan, defined a new product line (a digital 3 channel ECG Holter cardiac monitor), and received the American Food and Drug Administration (FDA) approval. In 1986 and in 1987, he received the "Approved Exporter Award," from Ariel Sharon, Minister of Industry and Trade.

Giora met with Ariel Sharon several times. The first time was in 1977 when he formed the Shlomtzion political party, a contraction of Shalom-Zion, or Peace-Zion and several times during 1984-7, while Sharon was Minister of Industry and Trade.

Sharon also thanked Giora in a letter (June 2, 1985) for his support during his libel law suit against Time magazine.

In addition to Ariel Sharon, Giora had met on various occasions with Prime Minister Shimon Peres, later the President of the State of Israel, Prime Minister Yitzhak Shamir, Health Minister Shoshanna Arbeli-Almozlino, and Minister of Energy and Infrastructure, Moshe Shahal.

Esther, Giora's Mother, passed away in 1986. Naturally, Giora took it hard as he was very close to his Mother. He used to send her postcards from all the places around the world. Giora learned from the neighbors how proud she was of him. She used to show everybody the articles written about his scientific achievements.

She was particularly proud of a small article published in the Hungarian "Uj-Kelet" (New East).

Uj-Kelet was a Zionist Jewish newspaper published in Hungarian which first appeared in Kolozsvár (Cluj) in Transylvania, Romania, and was later revived in Israel. Among the well-known writers in the newspaper, there were Rudolf Kastner, Yossef Lapid, and Ephraim Kishon.

Giora remembered the name frequently mentioned by his parents while they were still in Hungary and later in Israel.

It was Kishont Ferenc or as translated into Hebrew –Ephraim Kishon who immigrated to Israel in 1949 and became a famous Israeli writer.

Giora got divorced in 1986. He felt that his long and frequent absences from home were one of the major factors, but he couldn't change that. It was a quiet and respectful separation. His daughters took the new situation quite well; they met twice a week or whenever they wanted and he remained involved in their lives and studies.

Towards the end of 1987, the shareholders of the company decided to transfer operations to the U.S. and they let their subsidiary go. Giora left the company and started to inject new activities into his own company, Imexco General Ltd.

While visiting many hospitals worldwide, Giora identified the market need for an ambulatory Brain Monitor, similar to the one he had developed previously in Cardiology.

The existing systems were mainly analogue, bulky, expensive and very sophisticated to operate.

With a team of twenty two engineers, technicians and subcontractors, he developed unique proprietary technology for medical diagnostic monitoring equipment in the area of Neurology and Cardiology.

Instead of developing just one product, Giora decided to develop an entire platform or core technology to deal with physiological signals such as ECG and EEG.

Those core technologies were the basis for the successful development of a new digital ambulatory neuro-brain monitor – the Neuritor™, which is used for the acquisition and analysis of multi channel EEG signals in real - time.

The clinical applications of the Neuritor™ are quite diversified.

It is used for monitoring Parkinson's disease, Alzheimer, stroke, epilepsy, syncope, migraine, sleep investigations, psychogenic seizures, drug efficacy and transient ischemia of the brain.

It is an essential tool for monitoring brain activity during anesthesia in operating theatres, monitoring brain activity in intensive care units and cardiac care units. The Neuritor™ may be used for routine EEG examinations and for monitoring during surgery or intensive care, as well as situations which require a machine to be brought to the patient.

Giora believed that the market for self monitoring activities will expand as chronic care patients focus greater attention on preventive care.

Accordingly, he decided to invest in this exciting medical field.

In his effort to find partners for his unique project in Neurology, Giora approached the venture capital firm Athena headed by Dan Tolkowsky.

Tolkowsky had been a major general in the IDF, commander of the Israeli Air Force until 1958. He was involved in the Israeli nuclear project, and was a member of the IAEC. In 1985 he established Athena, a venture capital firm investing in high-tech projects.

During their first meeting in 1988 Tolkowsky was not excited about Giora's proposition and expressed doubts as to the feasibility of such a technological venture.

In fact he claimed that such miniaturization was impossible to perform with current technology.

He had bad advice from his technological consultants because after two years and 1.5 million dollars invested by Giora; the Neuritor received the American Food and Drug Administration (FDA) clearance to market it as an Electro-Encephalo-Graph (EEG) device.

In order to find partners and additional investments, Giora made a few trips to Europe and many more to the US.

The events that took place during one of those trips will never be forgotten by Giora.

It started well when he was upgraded to first class on a flight from Tel-Aviv to New York using his award points as a frequent flier with TWA. He was alone in first class until a group of security men boarded the plane with Shimon Peres, who was seated very close to Giora.

Peres and Giora had a short conversation, closely guarded by the security guards.

In Manhattan, Giora went straight to his attorney's office on Vanderbilt Avenue, near Grand Central station.

He was carrying a suitcase and small black attaché case.

When he left the office it was rush hour and it was difficult to get a cab, so Giora decided not to wait and went to the nearest bus station to go uptown. While waiting for the bus he was attacked in broad day light by two tall Afro-American men. They tried to steal his two cases. One was standing on his left and the other on his right. The people in the bus stop watched but said nothing and did nothing.

To protect his large suitcase on his right, Giora acted instinctively and broke the nose of the man on his right side with one blow with his strong left hand. At the same time the man on his left snatched his attaché case and disappeared. The guy with the broken nose cried out in pain, bleeding and fled in the opposite direction.

The entire scenario took just a few seconds. Giora was mugged, not the first time, but this was the first time he lost his case, which included, among other things, photos of Israeli officials, glasses, his passport, and airline tickets for the rest of the journey within the U.S. and back to Tel-Aviv, certain documents, a camera, an expensive fountain pen and other items.

As his attorney was quite well-known with the local authorities, the police officers from the precinct visited his attorney's place to take Giora's statement instead of the regular procedure of going downtown to the station.

The next day, at his attorney's office, while trying to contact the Israeli embassy for a new passport and TWA for a reissue of the airline tickets a very strange thing happened.

Someone from the post office in the borough of Queens called and asked for Giora.

They told him that they had found a bunch of things belonging to one Giora Ram in a plastic bag in a post box.

The next day Giora found almost everything in that bag, his passport, airline tickets, documents, and photos but not all the valuables and of course not the expensive leather attaché suitcase. Many times Giora asked himself whether the mugging had been random...

In 1992, Giora met a young, smart and a unique woman, and in 1993 they were married. It was a quiet and a modest wedding as her Mother had passed away just about a month earlier. Nine months later their son was born.

One of the products developed, the Neuritor-ST, was licensed to a subsidiary of the Israel Aircraft Industries. This subsidiary went public in the U.S. on the NASDAQ in 1993.

The technology, which was developed by the company for over five years, remained the proprietary ownership of Imexco General Ltd.

Another interesting innovative project that Giora worked on was a new product line in Pain Detection and Verification. This product, the Neuro-CPD™, has generated a lot of interest, not only among physicians and care takers, but also among insurance companies.

Only a few articles have been published about the seismic recording at Uppsala, Sweden, which referred to the strange Soviet nuclear test at Semipalitinsk.

One of the headlines was:

"Russia suspected of nuclear testing."

(*Washington Times*, August 28, 1997, *Washington Post*).

Another was:

"U.S. Suspects Russia set off Nuclear Test."

(The *New York Times*).

It was questionable whether it was a real nuclear explosion or an earthquake. The location was near the Russian Arctic nuclear test site at Novaya Zemlya. The officials in Moscow denied that any nuclear activity was involved. They claimed that it was a small earthquake in the Arctic Ocean east of Novaya Zemlya.

There are two theories on this subject. One is that the Russians devised a plan, which was probably adopted by others later on, to try to perform nuclear tests which coincided with or triggered an earthquake. The other theory is that the underground nuclear tests may have caused the earthquake.

In addition, scientists suspect that nuclear tests are weakening the earth's crust, triggering earthquakes and causing the earth's pole to shift.

During the period of 1995-2005 in addition to the scientific activities Giora performed for his company, he was engaged in business and technological consulting and served, among other capacities, as a business and technological advisor at several Israeli high-tech companies.

In 2005, thirteen happy years of marriage has ended, quietly and amicably, by mutual agreement.

In early 2006, Giora was selected by the US-Israel Science and Technology Foundation (USISTF), under their Technology Excellence Fellowship Program and spent several months at The Keck Center for Collaborative Neuroscience at Rutgers University, New Jersey, USA, where he conducted research related to spinal cord injury. It was a very rewarding and stimulating project. It was especially exciting to perform microsurgery on rats.

12. Military Technologies.

THE TECHNOLOGY base of most modern military applications is Digital Signal Processing (DSP).

The application areas include audio, speech and other sound data processing, sonar, radar, sensors, bio-medics, satellites, seismic data processing, telecommunication, missiles, and aviation.

Today almost every device has some kind of DSP chip embedded in its design. In cases of natural, real world signals, originally generated by analog mode, such as ECG or EEG in medical applications, they have to be converted to digital form in order to be processed and analyzed by computers.

Image Processing and Analysis in the 70s was a semi-classified research area.

Prof. Azriel Rosenfeld was one of the leading scientists in that area in the U.S.

He was a tenured Research Professor, a Distinguished University Professor, and Director of the Center for Automation Research at the University of Maryland in College Park, where he also held affiliate professorships in the Departments of Computer Science, Electrical Engineering, and Psychology.

He wrote the first textbook in the field in 1969 and was also the editor of the *International Journal of Computer Graphics and Image Processing*, in which Giora published two articles.

The first was in 1976, "Analysis of images specified by graph-like descriptions" and the second was in 1988, "On the encoding and representing of images."

The University of Southern California Signal and Image Processing Institute was one of the first research organizations in the world dedicated to image processing. This operation was funded by the Defense Advanced Research Projects Agency (DARPA).

Two leading scientists, William Pratt and Harry Andrews got their funds for the university.

The Internet was online in 1969 under the auspices of the Advanced Research Projects Agency (ARPA). Initially it connected four university computers in the southwestern US. It was named ARPANET.

Actually, it was designed to provide a communications network if some of the sites were destroyed by nuclear attack.

Technologies are applied for use in wars. The most famous technological equipment was the Enigma machine in use during WWII. The Germans developed several versions, but the Wehrmacht Enigma was used by the Nazi Germany during WWII. British Intelligence succeeded in deciphering a large number of messages which used the Enigma coding system. The claim was that it had a major impact and assisted the Allied war effort to end the war about two years earlier.

The technologies involved in developing military weapons or products are multi-leveled and have applications in myriad and diverse areas of operations. The deeper the level, the more sophisticated the technology is, but at the same times the usage is limited. The reason for such limitation is mainly because once it has been used; its mere existence has been disclosed. Those weapons or products are targeted mainly for surveillance and sabotage purposes.

They are developed and applied not only for use by the various units of the Israeli forces, but also for use by the enemy military forces, obviously without their knowledge.

In order to demonstrate the extent of such technology penetration into enemy activated weapons, here are few examples.

Let us assume that the enemy has a certain missile. They may have developed it themselves or bought it ready to use from another country. Each such a missile contains many components and today each has more than one onboard computer.

The sabotage involvements may be at the three stages: prior to launch, during the flight and upon reaching its target. We may consider that the target would be to destroy that missile if it is launched and aimed at Israel.

We also may consider changing or reprogramming its target coordinates, so that it would miss its target. We could consider sabotaging its operation so that it will not explode when reaching its target. We also may consider the option of "return to sender."

For each of the abovementioned options there are special technological solutions that enable achieving those goals. It is obvious that if the enemy starts receiving back its launched missiles, they will realize it quickly and stop using them. This option may be used just a very few times as the sabotage will be disclosed. Missing targets or non-exploding missiles are better solutions to eliminate this threat.

The question is how to achieve all that. The answer would be different for different types of weapons. The solutions are at different levels if the weapons are nuclear or conventional. In cases where the enemy is developing such weapons, the sabotage involvement is at multiple levels. There is involvement during development stages and involvement might be applied on the final product as well. Those involvements may be low level by simply planting specific electronic components developed by Israel up to the high level involvement, which may include the elimination of key individuals assisting in that development.

There are lower levels of involvement where the target is to delay and generate many obstacles during the development phases. In this category we may find a special unit, involved in "reverse engineering" of certain weapons used by the enemy.

If there is intelligence info about any such project to develop certain weapons, we can simulate the technical know-how required to achieve that goal and specifically find the list of components required for such a development.

Israel has the capability to supply those components not only at single source level but as second and even third source levels.

The following technologies, though they seem to be on the edge of science fiction, have already been developed and implemented or are in the research and development stage.

These technologies are used by the IDF in diverse applications, embedded in military equipment and weapons. Some of them are obviously top secret and their usage is limited to extreme scenarios. One should bear in mind that after such a class of equipment or weapons has been used, its existence is disclosed.

Here are partial list of those projects, products and capabilities:

- Developing marked and special electronic components to be used by manufacturers worldwide as part of specific military components and weapons. In this category we may see specific highly sophisticated dual and multi-core computers. The embedded preprogrammed processors can change and add certain functions upon remote or other triggered activation. They may transmit certain encoded information or change the main function of the device or weapon.

- Weapon activation by using Electro-Encephalo-Graph (EEG) connected to a pilot's special helmet. In addition, certain controls can be operated using eye movement.

  There are many other related projects at various stages of development which are used and will be used by the Israeli air force.

- Cryptography, codes deciphering and encrypted message transmissions. One of the interesting and practical application areas is "Quantum cryptography." Using photons, encrypted keys can be sent over a network of fiber optics. A key is created during the transmission of the message, while simultaneously the recipient scans the photons with a laser and interacts with the sender to generate a shared key for safe and secure transmission. External interference is immediately detected by an increase in error rate.

- Data Transmission from remote locations and products, which is triggered by remote signals, similar to GPS.

- The Americans followed the Russians for many years using photographic intelligence satellites. Those images provided vital information about Soviet strategic capabilities.

High resolution Satellite image data processing is a complex and sophisticated scientific research area. In the early 70s such data was used for civilian purposes as well as for military intelligence applications. New enhanced satellite imagery was and currently is in use by certain nations for diverse applications.

The TecSAR Israeli satellite - sometimes referred to as the Polaris or Ofek-8- was launched successfully on 21 January 2008. The Israeli satellite is capable of sending super high quality pictures in real-time.

Here is a quote from the Indian press: "India has successfully launched an Israeli spy satellite into orbit, officials at the Sriharikota space station in southern India." The Israeli press reported that the satellite would improve Israel's ability to monitor Iran's military activities. Indian officials reported that the operation was secret and carried out under tight security.

The TecSAR reconnaissance satellite, equipped with synthetic aperture radar, is said to have enhanced footage technology, which allows it to transmit images regardless of time of day and weather conditions. It is considered to be one of the most advanced spy satellites that India has put into orbit to date. Israeli newspapers reported that eighty minutes after launch, the Israel Aerospace Industries (IAI) ground station began receiving TecSAR's first signals. This 650-pound satellite is Israel's most advanced space craft.

It is equipped with top secret equipment, including a camera that can take pictures in almost any weather conditions. In addition, this kind of low-earth polar orbit enables Israel to closely monitor the Iranian nuclear program.

- Unique radar systems include a large range of diversified capabilities like the use of an Ultra Wide Band that can "see" through walls.

Dedicated radar systems integrated with reactive weapons that can calculate the origin of any kind of missile, its type, expected arrival time and location. This information is used to send the appropriate reaction to destroy an incoming missile well before it reaches its target. The missile range is expected to exceed 200 kilometers.

- Military implementations of certain nano-technologies, like smart miniaturized weapons with target-seeking ammunition are aimed at the destruction of infrastructures.

  A special application is the "nano suit", a bulletproof temperature controlled soldier suit that can also operate under water.

  Nanotechnology allows materials to be built up atom by atom. Military use of Nano-technologies using nano-materials can massively damage the lungs. Nano-particles can get into the body through the skin and may cause cell damage.

The most dangerous and powerful Nano-application is the Nano-bomb.
It contains self-multiplying engineered viruses that can wipe out an entire army by nano-poisoning.

- Robotics technologies are developed for diverse applications, such mobile mine and bomb detection and deactivation, unmanned vehicles and more.

- Neuroscience research has a wide range of uses for military applications, such as monitoring and affecting brain function and performance.

- Bio-engineering the brain aims at developing soldiers into "machines" or Cyborgs... This sounds like science-fiction. However, a similar program of generating a brain interface that will enable pilots to be wired to their plane is funded by the Defense Advanced Research Projects Agency.

- Laser and non-destructive testing use Holography technologies.

Dennis or Dénes Gábor in Hungarian was born on 5th of June 1900 in Budapest. He was a Hungarian electrical engineer and known for inventing holography, for which he received the Nobel Prize in Physics in 1971.

He escaped from Nazi Germany in 1933 to England. He worked at the British Thomson-Houston company and in 1947 he invented holography.

Laser technology developed rapidly enabling a variety of holographic applications in pattern recognition, art and data storage, and later in non-destructive testing. The Society for Photo-Optical Instrumentation Engineering (SPIE), which was named in 1981 as The International Society for Optical Engineering annually present the Dennis Gabor award for outstanding accomplishments in diffractive wave front technologies, with emphasis on new development of holography and metrology applications. Giora has been a member of SPIE since 1982.

Technology was and always will play a major role in preserving and protecting the national security of any nation.

In *The Crucible of Scientific Revolution*, Prof. Aharon Katchalsky (Katzir), describes the importance and the overall effect of the era of the scientific revolution.

This book, published in 1971, was quite novel for its time; Prof. Katzir, who worked on the electrochemistry of biopolymers and taught at the Hebrew University of Jerusalem, tells about various aspects of scientific evolution, such as morality and the place of science in our social life and discusses the dangers embedded in misuse of science.

Prof. Katzir was murdered in a terrorist attack at Ben Gurion (Lod) airport in 1972. His brother Ephraim was among "Heyl Mada" (HEMED) - scientific research and development corps founders involved in defense research at RAFAEL - the Armament Development Authority and other agencies. He was also a professor at the Weizmann Institute. In 1973 he became the fourth President of the State of Israel.

Just before he assumed office on the 24th of May 1973, Prof. Katzir held a farewell party from the Weizmann Institute and invited certain relatives, friends and students from the Institute.

At the party, Giora wished Katzir all the best in his new position and asked not to forget to advance scientific acceptance and better understanding among the civilians that he would be overseeing as President. Katzir responded with his famous half smile and said, "Sure!"

The CIA has a special report or review cable dedicated to Science and Weapons and they follow any significant development made in Israel closely.

Here are certain quotes from those classified documents released to the public on 10 January 1989.

SUBJECT: SCIENCE AND WEAPONS REVIEW CABLES. SW SWRC 89-5OO2K, 10 JANUARY 1989. THE ISRAELIS PROBABLY ARE MUCH MORE SERIOUS ABOUT DEVELOPING AN ATBM SYSTEM NOW THAN WHEN THEY BEGAN THEIR PROGRAM.

THEY UNDOUBTEDLY REALIZE THAT ARAB MISSILES ARMED WITH CHEMICAL WARHEADS HAVE COME TO POSE A MAJOR THREAT.

ISRAELIS SHOULD BE ABLE TO MEET THEIR 1995 DEPLOYMENT GOAL FOR THE ARROW. TO OBTAIN INITIAL TARGET POSITION AND VELOCITY DATA, THE ARROW WILL RELY ON A PHASED-ARRAY RADAR. AFTER TARGET TRACK BY THE RADAR, THE ARROW WILL BE LAUNCHED.

IT WILL USE GROUND-BASED RADAR DERIVED DATA FOR THE INITIAL PORTION OF THE FLIGHT. AN ONBOARD MEASUREMENT UNIT THEN WILL FLY IT TO THE ESTIMATED INTERCEPT POINT. TARGET KILL WILL BE AFFECTED BY A NONNUCLEAR, SHAPED WARHEAD. THE PLANNED PROBABILITY OF KILL IS 90 PERCENT.

THE PROTOTYPE OF THE HYPERVELOCITY GUN HAS A BARREL ABOUT 4 METERS LONG, ABOUT 45 CM IN DIAMETER IN THE REAR, AND TAPERING TO ABOUT 18 CM IN FRONT.

PROPULSION IS STARTED BY ELECTRO-MAGNETIC FORCE FOLLOWED BY A CHEMICAL CHARGE TO INCREASE VELOCITY. THE SYSTEM HAS ACHIEVED A VELOCITY OF 1,950 METERS PER SECOND.

THE TESTS HAVE BEEN CONDUCTED AT THE SOREQ NUCLEAR RESEARCH FACILITY SOUTH OF TEL AVIV. THE FINAL GUN PROBABLY WILL HAVE A CALIBER OF ABOUT 155 MILLIMETERS.

ISRAEL HAS AN EXTENSIVE LASER RESEARCH AND DEVELOPMENT COMMUNITY. THERE ARE 35 ISRAELI FIRMS, AS WELL AS A NUMBER OF UNIVERSITIES, ENGAGED IN ELECTRO-OPTICS AND LASER RESEARCH AND PRODUCTION. THE CENTER OF EXCELLENCE FOR CHEMICAL LASERS AT BEN GURION UNIVERSITY HAS A GRANT UNDER TUE SDI FRAMEWORK TO DEVELOP NOVEL CHEMICAL LASERS.

SOURCE REPORTING INDICATES THAT THE WEAPON SYSTEMS DIVISION OF RAFAEL, THE ISRAELI ARMS DEVELOPMENT AUTHORITY, IS WORKING ON AN AIRBORNE CHEMICAL LASER WEAPON SIMILAR TO THE U.S. MIRCL SYSTEM.

GIVEN THE DIFFICULTIES THE UNITED STATES HAS ENCOUNTERED IN TRYING TO DEVELOP LASERS FOR MISSILE DEFENSE, WE BELIEVE THAT THE ISRAELI AIRBORNE HEL WILL BE MORE USEFUL AGAINST CRUISE MISSILES THAN AGAINST BALLISTIC MISSILES.

SPACE BASED SENSORS. WITH THE LAUNCH OF THEIR FIRST SATELLITE, THE ISRAELIS DEMONSTRATED THEIR CAPABILITY TO PLACE A SATELLITE IN LOW EARTH ORBIT.

ISRAEL: ANTITACTICAL BALLISTIC MISSILE PROGRAM. VARIOUS SOURCES INDICATE THAT THE ISRAELIS ARE ENGAGED IN A LARGE DIVERSE ANTITACTICAL BALLISTIC MISSILE (ATBM) PROGRAM TO DEVELOP DEFENSES AGAINST ARAB MISSILES ARMED WITH CHEMICAL WARHEADS.

ACCORDING TO THESE SOURCES, THE ISRAELIS PLAN TO HAVE THE FIRST PHASE OF THESE DEFENSES READY BY 1995. A LARGE PART OF THEIR ATBM PROGRAM IS FUNDED THROUGH THE U.S. STRATEGIC DEFENSE INITIATIVE (SDI) PROGRAM.

13. Governments and Terrorism.

"Government of the people, by the people,
for the people, shall not perish from the earth."

UNFORTUNATELY, these days those words and goals are still not implemented and probably never will be. There are too many interests involved in establishing such an ideal government. Too much ego, prejudice, and economic, social and many other and conflicting interests are involved in the basic ingredients for melding such a government. Maybe it should be like this in the name of democracy and freedom of choice; maybe the people don't deserve such an ideal government.

The major problem is generating the desired balance among all those ideals and desires. The two extreme possibilities are a government with too much power and a weak, divided government that is unable to make crucial decisions. A government or an organization with enough resources can do almost anything.

Not only that, they can even publicly justify their actions in the name of preserving and protecting the democracy. They will support their actions, which may be illegal, immoral or even criminal in the name of justice, for the people and nation. To balance between a completely open society where everything is transparent, visible and known to everybody and a closed society where certain actions and information are known to few is a very difficult task. "People don't have to know everything," may have justification in certain cases. Polls have already proved that the mood of people can be easily manipulated and change directions with time, events and publicity. Governments can, if they wish, eliminate certain groups or individuals who, in their opinion, oppose and are hostile to their policies. The elimination of a terrorist or a political opponent is as easy to achieve as it is easy to hide from the public. The death or disappearance of such people is explained under categories such as natural causes, accidents, mental hospitalization or death during emergency surgery.

All agencies, unofficial and official, such as the CIA, MI5/6, KGB and the Mossad, were and will be doing "it" in the name of national security. The popular public reason may be: "In order to protect, preserve or even enforce Democracy." In certain cases those actions might be truly justified; the problem is where to set the limit. Many people have disappeared worldwide in the name of national security.

The reason of national security for not disclosing certain information or imprisoning an undesired subject is used too often by many countries and organizations.

Governments operate mainly at three levels. While level one is the clean and white level of activities, reserved for heads of states and highly exposed political figures, level two is the gray area. This is an unethical area of activity which smells bad but is still legal. Killing, eliminating, removing and falsifying are part of level three. Normally, "we the people" are exposed to level one and occasionally to level two, but rarely to level three.

At level three, I can mention for example, Gerald Bull, the Canadian engineer who developed the Babylon or "super-gun" long-range artillery for the Iraqi government. Bull was assassinated in Brussels, Belgium in March 1990.

It is quite interesting to note the language evolution with regard to using politically correct terminologies. The word-laundering is quite fascinating. Terms such as "Terrorists" or "freedom fighters," "guerillas", "political assassination" or "removing from power" all depends on which side you ask or talk to.

The USA is a super-power with worldwide presence and intervention. In general, they are a stabilizing factor. Many Americans don't understand the importance of their support for certain countries and at the same time many supported countries simply hate their presence.

To better understand the above, try to imagine a world without the U.S. involvement. Let's assume that the U.S. is not a super-power or they evolved from an Empire to a regular Republic interested mainly in their internal affairs.

What would the world look like without U.S. intervention?

Oil is one of the major energy resources of most modern countries. Oil was one of the main reasons for wars and the invasion of Kuwait by Saddam Hussein. It was not a territorial dispute; it was about oil. The Americans are one of the largest oil consumers, so it is obvious why the U.S. was interested in assisting Kuwait. However, this is not the whole picture. The U.S. involvement all over the world is not only for oil and monetary interests. Most people believe that there are other reasons. In the era of a globalized economy, world stability is essential and according to the Chaos theory, even a small problem in the Middle-East, for example, can generate a chain reaction which affects the U.S. in many areas. Most people believe that the global American intervention is also because they care. They care about establishing and maintaining Democracies and enabling freedom for everybody everywhere possible. Obviously there are other reasons and interests; so what are they?

China is becoming a major player in the world arena. They are the second largest oil consumers. The route of oil to China is secured and enabled by the U.S. Navy. China's long term goal might be to be equal the U.S. and they can achieve it.

Without the U.S., Taiwan would cease to exist as a Democracy and may be annexed to mainland China. Without the U.S., Japan would have to get nuclear capabilities if they wanted to remain independent. They have had a continuing dispute with China since 1937, and the Chinese will never forget the Japanese invasion. The U.S. assisted Iran indirectly by eliminating Saddam Hussein, who had fought Iran over a border dispute for eight years. Saddam Hussein was interested in making Iraq an influential power in the Persian Gulf region. He invaded Iran not only because of the long history of border disputes, but also to enlarge Iraq's oil reserves. Europe wants and needs oil, but they are not willing to pay the full price to get it. They hate the American presence and will not acknowledge that without the U.S., they wouldn't get the oil they need.

Europe's attitude toward Israel is extremely hypocritical. They have a short memory; however what unites Europe against Israel or the Jews is Anti-Semitism.

Since March 2003 when Recep Tayyip Erdogan became Turkey's Prime Minister, their policy toward Israel has changed. Erdogan was unhappy with Israel's reaction to Hezbollah's kidnapping of soldiers in 2006; he was critical when Israel conducted the Gaza War; he asked to inspect Israel's nuclear facilities under IAEA inspection; and he has criticized Israel for its many defensive actions.

The tension between the countries has escalated following the Gaza flotilla raid.

The question is what his motives are and if he has a hidden agenda that may explain his overzealous attention to Israel. His reactions have gained Turkey influence and sympathy among his Arab neighbors. Particularly, he may have gained certain advantages among his domestic political parties. His special collaborative attention and meetings with Syria and Iran should worry the West and particularly Israel.

The Kurdistan Workers' Party or PKK, founded in 1978, is a Kurdish organization which fights against Turkey. Their goal is to establish an independent Kurdish state.

There is a claim by Germany that the Turkish military has used chemical weapons against members of the PKK.

Lebanon is a puppet country controlled by Syria and Iran. Hezbollah or "The Party of God" is a Shi'a Islamic organization involved in Lebanese politics, supported by Syria and Iran. Actually, they are viewed by most of the world as a terrorist organization.

Their forces are trained and organized by the Iranian Revolutionary Guards. Their main goal is to eliminate the colonial entity in Lebanon and to establish an Islamic regime.

To achieve that, the Iranians with their supporters all are united under the hatred towards Israel and their desire to eliminate the Zionist entity from the region.

A top secret CIA document released on April 2004 lists the many possible suspects for the assassination of Elie Hobeika, former Lebanese Forces Commander.

Possible culprits include fellow Christians, other members of the Lebanese elite, Palestinians and Israelis.

According to a Western news agency, a previously unknown anti-Syrian group, "Lebanese for a Free and Independent Lebanon." has claimed responsibility. The claim may be associated with rightwing Maronite Christians, who bore a grudge against Hobeika because he betrayed the Lebanese Forces and the Israelis by switching allegiance to the Syrians in the mid-80. Hobeika also was active in Christian infighting during Lebanon's civil war.

Palestinians despise Hobeika because he allegedly directed the massacre of approximately 1,000 Palestinians in the refugee camps of Sabra and Shatilla in 1992.

An Israeli commission in 1983 accused Hobeika of carrying out the massacre and held then Defense Minister Ariel Sharon indirectly responsible for the attack.

Many Lebanese suspect Israeli involvement because Hobeika had said he would testify against Sharon if the Belgians went forward with a trial accusing Sharon of genocide and crimes against humanity for his role in Sabra and Shatilla.

A Belgian court next month will rule on whether a judicial investigation into Sharon's role can proceed.

President Lahud claims Hobeika was killed to stop him from testifying, according to press reports, a sentiment echoed by other government officials.

There is no direct evidence of Israeli involvement in the assassination, but highlighting an Israeli connection could help the Lebanese avoid the internal friction that would arise if a Lebanese group were blamed.

Anybody who thinks that the Israel-Palestinian conflict is over territories is totally wrong.

Israelis are willing to give back certain territories and make peace in exchange for a piece of paper... Unfortunately, based on history, those signed agreements have a very short life time. In the volatile region of the Middle-East Israel will face many difficulties without U.S. support. In the 1980s Soviet military forces in Afghanistan faced a different type of war than they had experienced in the past. The resistance forces fighting them were the *mujahedeens*.

The Makhtab Al-Khidamat (MAK) was founded by Osama Bin Laden and Abdullah Azzam, which led to the establishment of Al-Qaeda in 1988. At the end of the Soviet occupation they wanted to extend and justify their operations, so they tried to include other Islamic causes. It is quite obvious that Al-Qaeda benefited from the U.S. funding and training given to the Afghan mujahedeen fighting the Soviet invasion. There are many Al-Qaeda cells which are operative worldwide. Without united cooperation they will continue their terrorist operations including their attempt to get nuclear related weapons.

14. Nuclear Projects, Policies & Threats.

THE NPT or Nuclear Non-Proliferation Treaty is an agreement to limit the spread of nuclear weapons; it was initiated in 1968. India, Israel, Pakistan and North Korea are not parties to the treaty. While India, Pakistan and North Korea have openly tested and admitted that they have nuclear weapons, Israel has had a vague policy regarding its nuclear capabilities and possession of such weapons.

The articles of the NPT consist mainly of three elements: non-proliferation, disarmament, and the right to use nuclear technology for peaceful applications.

Israel has been developing nuclear weapons at its site in Dimona, previously known as a textile factory, since 1958. It is estimated that Israel may have between 200 to 400 warheads.

The arsenal includes thermonuclear weapons, designed by Edward Teller and Stanislaw Ulam in 1951 and strategic warheads in the megaton range.

The following section is a quote from a top secret CIA document from the eighties approved for release only on January 2004.

The quote is only a small part of the entire document, which was mostly blackened and remains classified.

The driving force behind Israel's nuclear program is national security. The bombing of Iraq's Osirak reactor in 1981 illustrates Israel's determination to maintain a monopoly on nuclear weapons in the Middle East.

Israel, which began nuclear research as soon as it became a state in 1948, has the most advanced nuclear technology in the Middle East.

Although it would like to buy nuclear power plants, which would be much cheaper than building its own, questions about its nuclear weapons program have limited cooperation with nuclear suppliers. Concern among potential suppliers over Arab reaction to cooperation with Israel has also been a problem for Israel.

The Israel Atomic Energy Commission (IAEC) is the principal national authority concerned with nuclear policy and program administration. Attached to the Office of the Prime Minister, the IAEC manages the nation's research facilities and programs with the assistance of relevant government ministries such as Defense, Foreign Affairs, Science and Development, and Energy and infrastructure.

The IAEC has 20 commissioners, largely former senior government officials, who sit on the main board, the apex of the IAEC's structure. They are responsible for policy support to the commission.

Despite Israeli claims that the Defense Ministry has little or no involvement in the nuclear program, the Ministry almost certainly plays a role in the country's nuclear activities. We believe the IAEC and the Defense Ministry operate in tandem.

Whatever its relationship with the Defense Ministry, the IAEC has a sizable internal bureaucracy that deals with various nuclear activities, including the day-to-day operations of Israel's two research reactors.

IAEC's bureaucratic structure consists of a director general, a deputy director general several advisory subcommittees, and at least three functional divisions. We estimate that the overall IAEC scientific and technical staff totals 300 to 400 personnel.

Prime Minister Yitzhak Shamir is chairman of the IAEC and has final authority over nuclear policy. He professes to oppose the proliferation of nuclear weapons and has called for the creation of a nuclear-free zone in the Middle East. Nevertheless, like previous Israeli leaders, he has refused to sign the NPT, noting that Israel would compromise its nuclear capabilities if it were forced to open all its facilities to IAEA inspection. Moreover, Shamir has never dismissed the possibility of an Israeli nuclear deterrent to counter the conventional forces of Israel's Arab neighbors.

Because Israel 1acks natural energy resources, primarily oil, Shamir supports the development of nuclear power reactor. Israel has a 4,750-MW electrical generating capacity, but no electricity is produced by nuclear power.

Israel has researched the feasibility of nuclear power and has chosen a site in the Negev desert for a future nuclear plant. The Israel Electrical Corporation estimates that Israel will not need a nuclear plant until the year 2000. Tel Aviv's research has concluded that it would be less expensive for Israel to acquire foreign nuclear power technology than to produce its own power reactors.

Israel has no uranium deposits, but since the early 1970s it has been recovering uranium from phosphate deposits in the Negev desert. Uranium recovery is almost certainly sufficient to permit the continuing operation of the Dimona reactor, which probably consumes no more than 20 to 30 tons of uranium per year.

Israel's refusal to sign the NPT and to put all its nuclear installations under IAEA safeguards has severely limited nuclear cooperation with other countries. For instance, Israel has successfully approached several countries, including the Unites States, Canada, France, Spain, the United Kingdom, and West Germany, to purchase a nuclear reactor and nuclear technology.

Serious discussions developed only with France,
but Paris pulled out of the negotiations because of
concerns about damage to its relations with
important Arab trading partners.

John von Neumann or in Hungarian Neumann János Lajos was born on December 28th, 1903 in Budapest of the Austro-Hungarian Empire to wealthy Jewish parents, Margit (Margaret) and Miksa (Max) Neumann.

His father, a lawyer, was working in a bank. He was a Hungarian American mathematician who made major contributions to a vast range of fields, including: functional analysis, quantum mechanics, set theory, economics and game theory, computer science, numerical analysis, hydrodynamics, and many other mathematical fields.

The application of operator theory to quantum mechanics and the development of functional analysis were pioneered by Von Neumann.

He was a principal member of the Manhattan Project.

Von Neumann together with Edward Teller and Stanislaw Ulam, an American mathematician of Polish-Jewish origin, developed the nuclear physics process involved in thermonuclear reactions and the hydrogen bomb, which was called the Teller–Ulam design of thermonuclear weapons.

Von Neumann is regarded as one of the greatest mathematicians in modern history. His brilliance stood out among other known Hungarian Jewish scientists. These included Theodore von Kármán, a physicist who was active in the fields of aeronautics and astronautics, Eugene (Jenő) Wigner a physicist and mathematician, Leó Szilárd, a physicist who conceived the idea of the nuclear chain reaction in 1933 and patented the idea of a nuclear reactor with Enrico Fermi and, of course, Edward Teller. Edward Teller, or Ede in Hungarian, was born in Budapest on January 15, 1908 to an educated and affluent Jewish family. Teller, a Nobel Prize winner, is best known for his work on the American nuclear program, and specifically as a member of the Manhattan Project during World War II.

Teller was in Israel many times after his meeting with David Ben-Gurion in 1952. He was a major contributor to the Israeli nuclear program and cooperated with Yuval Neeman. Prof. Neeman was a distinguished theoretical physicist and colonel in the IDF. Between 1961 and 1963 he was the director of Nachal Soreq and later the president of Tel Aviv University. From 1966, for 26 years he was member and acting chairman of IAEC and in the 80s he was Minister of Science.

During his visits, Teller met with key individuals in the government and Israel's security forces and expressed his views and recommendations with regard to the right way to develop nuclear capabilities. He expressed his strong disagreement to the NPT treaty and recommended not signing it.

The CIA and the American government were aware of Teller's activities in Israel and they were informed about the progress Israel had made in the nuclear area.

According to the foreign Press, the policy of ambiguity was maintained for many years by the Israeli government.

Accordingly, they will not confirm or deny the possession of nuclear weapons.

This policy was somewhat violated by Mordechai Vanunu, a technician at the Negev Nuclear Research Center, who revealed certain nuclear related secrets to the British press in 1986. The nuclear issue has become a major headache and concern to the free world. Iran is the major cause for this concern, but also of concern is North Korea, who has threatened to restart their nuclear program. There is a united effort made towards a world free from nuclear weapons.

The CIA and the Mossad have been cooperating for a long time on a top secret program to sabotage Iran's development of their nuclear program by persuading key individuals to defect. If persuasion doesn't work, they are eliminated. Nuclear physicists are the focus of this international effort. Iraqi nuclear scientists were recruited during visits to France for various reasons. In this case they were good sources for gathering information about Iraq's nuclear reactor Osiraq (Tamuze 17), which was destroyed in 1981 by the Israeli Air Force.

In recent years, we hear about "disappearing acts" quite often and probably there are more cases that are unpublicized. Shahram Amiri was an Iranian nuclear scientist from Qom, Iran. He worked at a heavily-guarded underground site at Qom. He also taught physics, radiation and isotope technology at Malek Ashtar University in Tehran.

In addition, Amiri was employed by Iran's Atomic Energy Organization (IAEO) and known to be involved in Iran's nuclear program. Amiri was a very bright young nuclear physicist in his late 30s. He spoke English very well and was quite westernized. He vanished during a pilgrimage to Mecca in Saudi Arabia in May 2009. The Iranians accused the U.S. government of being involved in his disappearance.

Another suggestion was that he wanted to seek asylum abroad. This suggestion is supported by a certain intelligence agency which claimed Amiri actually defected with the assistance of the CIA. The CIA had contacted Amiri when he visited Frankfurt in relation to his scientific research work.

There he met a German business man with whom he traveled to Vienna for the purpose of assisting a certain Iranian individual associated with the International Atomic Energy Agency (IAEA).

Shortly afterwards he flew to Mecca and hasn't been seen since.

Only four months after Amiri's disappearance, President Barack Obama disclosed that Iran had built the underground uranium enrichment plant near the holy city of Qom. Amiri's first hand knowledge about Qom's plant layout and security procedures were no doubt vital information to IAEA. Amiri had defected to the US, but in July 2010 he voluntarily returned to Iran.

Another vanishing act was performed by General Ali Reza Asgari, former commander of Iran's Revolutionary Guard, who vanished during a trip to Turkey in 2007. According to *The Sunday Times*, Asgari was recruited during a business trip in 2003.

It is not clear which intelligence agency recruited him, but Iranian officials claim that it was the CIA with the Mossad's collaboration.

Massoud Ali Mohammadi was an Iranian professor of nuclear physics, who was killed by a bomb in Tehran on January 12, 2010. He was a professor at Tehran University.

He taught neutron physics and was the author of articles on quantum and theoretical physics published in several scientific journals. Iranian officials have obviously accused Israel and the United States of being behind the assassination.

In recent years, unobserved by the eyes of governments such as Britain, France, Germany and others, cells of terrorism are flourishing. Intelligence agencies of these countries are no doubt aware of these underground activities. Unfortunately, they are doing absolutely nothing about it. The problem is that they don't understand that type of activity and don't interpret correctly and soon it will be too late. Many times they have ignored illegal and potentially dangerous activities in the name of being politically correct.

During WWII nothing was sacred. According to Churchill, the soft belly of Europe was Italy. Accordingly, they also bombed Monasteries such as Monte Casino in Italy.

The allies launched attacks and bombed indiscriminately. They left behind massive destruction of bridges, railroads and power stations. WWII exposed human hatred and cruelty. In these days, the countries that executed those atrocities together with countries that suffered most from them criticize Israel in her attempt to defend herself. The world has a short memory. People don't realize the existence of historical cycles. It should be remembered that "What goes around comes around."

Groups of people that refuse to acknowledge opinions different from theirs, or won't acknowledge their opponents in culture, race or any other area or field will attempt to eliminate those opponents. They will do so in the name of Allah, Jesus or any other God. The need to involve religion with politics is well known throughout history and it is a very dangerous combination. One of the reasons they involve God in their fights and wars is to unify the largest number of active and non-active supporters for the cause, whatever it may be.

On a small scale, let us assume that in a small village somewhere, people have blond, black, red and white hair. The people with the four hair colors are equally distributed in the village, so each group has about the same number of people.

The blonds don't like the blacks. The blacks don't like the whites and nobody likes the reds, creating complete harmony...

The only thing that united the blacks, reds and whites is their religion; they believe in EGO God Almighty, while the Blonds have AGO as God. In their village two houses to worship their Gods were built, one for EGO and one for AGO.

All the villagers have small farms, the same land using the same water well. The blonds are more creative and invest their knowledge, money and energy into their farms, working day and night with their spouses in the fields. The rest of the villagers are lazy, smoking pipes and playing cards; only their women work in the fields.

One day two neighbors, a blond and a black had a dispute over garden pests.

It was nothing serious and it should have been resolved quickly and amicably, but it escalated into a big fight involving some of the black and blond neighbors as well.

The reds and the whites just smiled, as both peoples were indifferent to the conflict and anyhow they didn't like either the blacks or the blonds.

The case was brought to court and a jury of an equal number of blonds, blacks, whites and reds was selected.

During trial, the blond farmer claimed that snakes, scorpions and other pests were coming from his black neighbor's farm, destroying his garden, entering his house and endangering his children.

He asked his black neighbor several times to take care of this inconvenience, but the neighbor just ignored him. In order to avoid further escalation, the blond decided to build a fence, which he did.

Now the black is suing and asking to bring down the fence, as it disturbs his view and he cannot walk through his neighbor's yard as he did before.

When it was obvious that the judge and the jury were going to support the claims made by the blond, the black made his last attempt to win his case. He claimed that he was unable to worship EGO because of the fence.

He also claimed that the blond not only didn't believe in EGO, but he was cursing almighty God. In addition, the implication for all other villagers might be that all blonds would build fences and this would cause difficulties for worshiping EGO. The cause of religion united the majority of the jury against the blond and he lost the case.

As long as it was a local dispute over small neighborly related civilian issue, it could be resolved by the parties. However, when it became a religious issue, it involved and united all villagers. Israel is the "glue" that unites most Muslims.

Nobody can understand in depth the Arab mentality better than their Israeli cousins. Arabs adore power and at the same time they despise fear. They would go very far in order to achieve their goals, especially if it is supported by their religious leaders.

In civilized western countries, signed agreements have value. Well, not exactly. The Munich Pact, which was signed on September 30, 1938 by Chamberlain and Hitler, had no value at all.

When Joachim von Ribbentrop, the German Foreign Minister, was very unhappy about it, the Führer replied, "Don't take it so seriously. That piece of paper has no significance whatever."

Another "piece of paper," which may have some historical value, was sent to the British Prime Minister, Harold Macmillan, on June 2, 1961 by the Secretary of State for Foreign Affairs, Alec Douglas-Home. It was classified as secret, and stated that:

I saw Mr. Ben Gurion this afternoon and told him of our concern about the Israel nuclear reactor in the Negev. Mr. Ben Gurion explained that its object was to train personnel in preparation for an atomic energy programme in 10 or 15 years' time aimed at providing cheap power for taking the salt out of sea water to irrigate the Negev.

I asked Mr. Ben Gurion whether he could not accept international inspection and safeguards. Mr. Ben Gurion said that he did not think he could since this would mean bringing in the Russians and the Arabs. But he might be prepared to accept inspection by neutrals.

Mr. Ben Gurion pressed his case for defensive missiles which he told me he had discussed with you this morning. He was particularly concerned about the fact that the Israelis had no counter to the MIG 19. Mr. Ben Gurion was anxious for an early reply. I told him that I would discuss the matter with you but that while I saw the strength of his case, I shared your fear of starting a missile race.

The British concern about the Israeli nuclear reactor in the Negev was much more than just "concern" as put very politely by the British Intelligence. A detailed prior document labeled "Top Secret" for "U.K. Eyes Only" from the 8th of February 1960 indicates that they were very much concerned and troubled about the possibility of Israel having nuclear capabilities.

Here are some quotes from that document entitled: "Secret Atomic Activities in Israel":

Israel has an atomic programme which dates back to 1948 and which is administered by an Atomic Energy Commission (A.E.C.) coming under the Prime Minister's office, Most of the publicized activity related to research where the Israeli effort is quite impressive.

The research centres round the Weizmann Institute at Rehovoth, near which there is a small American reactor of no military Significance.

The declared activity and aims of the Israeli A.E.C. are entirely non-military and there are only individual points which appear suspicious. The chief point might be considered the Rehovoth Conference of 1960 where leading scientists from many countries were given a picture of Israeli activities which omitted all reference to the Beersheba site.

The Israelis also maintain a lively interest in the industrial production of heavy water which seems somewhat out of phase with the lack of any firm overt project for building a reactor.

It is also noteworthy that Ernst Bergmann, Chairman of the Israeli A.E.C., simultaneously heads the scientific department of the Ministry of Defence and that the Weizmann Institute reactor referred to above was erected with the help of the Ministry of Defence.

To prove the existence of military interest in the Israeli nuclear program the document indicates that:

In 1958 two new appointments were reported in the Israeli Ministry of Defence. Major-General Dan Tolkowsky, previously A.O.C. Israeli Air Force, became responsible to the Minister of Defence and the Chief of Staff for coordinating the services' requirements from industry; this post was also described as including responsibility for atomic research. At the same time Meir Maridor, previously Director of Development Projects was made Head of an Authority for the Development of Means of Warfare in the Ministry of Defence.

In April 1959 Chancery in Tel Aviv reported a reference by Shimon Peres, Director General of the Ministry of Defence to Israeli efforts to obtain a secret weapon (unspecified).

Peres was said, about the same time, to be extremely keen to have a nuclear weapon, and confident that the French would supply it; he was also critical of the theoretical nature of the work of the Weizmann Institute.

Tolkowsky, on the other hand, had apparently been commissioned to review Israel's atomic policy and his conclusion, backed by the majority of military opinion, was that it would be wise to keep the Middle East free of nuclear weapons.

The Israeli Prime Minister thought that Israel ought to concentrate first on a reactor for power production but might later achieve a nuclear weapon of her own.

According to xxxxxxxx a Franco-Israeli agreement on atomic matters was concluded in 1956. Under its terms the French undertook to help Israel to build in the Negev a research centre including a "powerful" reactor. Within French Government circles the Prime Minister alone knew all the details of the agreement with Israeli and even the Foreign Minister was only generally aware of it.

Four main conclusions emerge:

(i) There has been secret Franco-Israeli collaboration on atomic energy.

(ii) The site near Beersheba, described is indeed an atomic site, including a reactor, and probably equates with the research institute to be built under a Franco-Israeli agreement.

(iii) At present the Beersheba site does not resemble a complex for producing fissile material. Unless the Marcoule type reactor, mentioned in the France-Israeli agreement, together with a plutonium reparation plant are already well-advanced at some other secret Israeli site (and this seems doubtful) Israel does not have any fissile material and will not have any for at least two years, which we estimate to be the minimum period required to add the appropriate facilities to the Beersheba site.

(iv) There are indications that, despite the Franco-Israeli agreement, French and Israeli ideas about Israeli atomic programme may be different. For instance the Israelis did not wish to publicize their agreement with France; and they have sought advice and assistance outside France.

It is not possible at this stage to offer any firm opinion as to ultimate Israeli intentions. More yet needs to be found out; and above all it is necessary to find out what arrangements are envisaged for the processing of the reactor fuel from present or future Israeli reactors. If this fuel is to be treated in Israeli or, alternatively, if it is to be treated in France but the plutonium extracted is to be returned to Israel without safeguards, then Israel will begin to accumulate fissile material from which nuclear weapons could be made.

Assuming that the Beersheba reactor is so far the only sizeable reactor in Israel (this seems likely) and assuming further that it is a big heavy water reactor (this we do not know) it could make enough plutonium for, says six nuclear weapons a year.

The "Marcoule" type reactor, for which the Israelis were to buy blueprints, would provide plutonium for up to twelve nuclear weapons a year.

The Hungarian connection to nuclear related activities was monitored and documented by the CIA. In a secret document dated 14 October 1959 that was released only in June 2005, it was reported that the CIA was following the uranium mining in Hungary closely. The uranium was processed in the USSR.

Uranium mining in Hungary started in 1956, when uraniferous sandstone deposits were discovered by Soviet and Hungarian exploration teams in the Pécs area. At that time, expeditions were set up to explore for uranium deposits throughout Hungary, and a joint Soviet-Hungarian uranium mining stock company was formed over which the Soviets have complete control.
This company is known as the Bauxite Mining Enterprises with headquarters believed to be in Budapest.

The Enterprise is subordinate to the Number 2 Section of the Hungarian Ministry of Chemical Industry and Electric Power. This Section is also called the Uranium Planning Office, and is located at 16 Munkasi Mihaly Ut., Budapest.

Uranium deposits in the Pécs area consist mostly of Paleozoic, Mesozoic, sad Tertiary sedimentary rocks, which have been folded and slightly faulted. The uranium deposits are in light-reddish marine sandstones and are widely dispersed. The mountains are of low and hilly relief. Some of the deposits are quite similar to those found in the U.S. Colorado Plateau.

Reportedly, uranium ore is mined in two main areas in Hungary: the vicinity of Pécs, and at Bakonya. The reported mining areas include Kovagoszollos near Pécs (46°05'N-18°05'E) where three mines are also in operation; Balatonfüred, Veszprém Kaposvar, Miskolc, Bataszek and at Lake Balaton and Meczek.

It is believed that a uranium processing plant was built near Pécs during 1958, although no information is as yet available on its size or processes used.

Although the proven Hungarian uranium reserves are quite extensive, they are being exploited at a relatively slow rate by the Soviets.

In 1957, the first year of full production, ore containing approximately 100 tons of recoverable uranium metal was produced. In the next few years it is estimated that Hungary will produce ore containing up to perhaps 1000 tons of recoverable uranium metal per year.

All the output of Hungarian uranium mines is sent to the USSR for reduction to metal.

15. U.S.S.R. Spies Exposed.

THE COLLAPSE of the Soviet Union commenced in the early 1980s. The inevitable direction was obvious in 1985 and the final collapse came in 1991 when Boris Yeltsin seized power. During that chaotic period, a large amount of weapons, merchandise and money exchanged hands. Some people were killed and some got rich; a few became known as oligarchs.

Money is a weapon. With money you can buy a small country or destroy its economy. The Israeli Financial Intelligence Unit (FIU) was established to assist in the investigation and prevention of money laundering and terror financing related to criminal activities.

A dysfunctional banking system, irrational or inconsistent policy making or the lack of protection for freedom of business may be elements which cause economic disaster. For example, the easy provision of mortgages to borrowers with insufficient collateral was one of the main causes of the global financial crisis.

Israel has had an open flow of goods and capital since the early 1990s when the government adopted a new economic policy of liberalization of foreign exchange control. Therefore policymakers for both fiscal and monetary policy have to carefully monitor the capital flow as the exchange rate fluctuates rapidly.

The Israeli real-estate market did not experience the same price increases that were seen in the US, the UK and Europe.

Accordingly, the banks in Israel were much less exposed to such risk. Israeli financial institutions, such as mutual fund management companies, are relatively small and their assets primarily include domestic financial assets and government bonds. Therefore, their exposure to the influence of the global market and securities was relatively small. The global financial crisis has affected the Israeli financial system by an increase in volatility and uncertainty in Israel's capital markets. The enemies of Israel are aware of Israel's economic volatility and they have attempted not once to use it as another frontier to attack Israel.

With the fall of the Soviet Union, archives were opened to reveal a huge amount of secret intelligence information, especially about spies, double agents and sleepers.

Dimitri was a former KGB agent who saw his colleagues making a lot of money. It took him a while to realize what they are selling. Giora met Dimitri a few times in the past on various occasions. There was mutual understanding and respect between the two.

They found out that their fathers had shared a similar background while "spending" some time in Siberia. They also shared a very similar physique, strong arms and wide shoulders.

In winter of 1985, Giora was on a flight from Frankfurt to Tokyo with a short stopover at Moscow's international airport. In the duty free shop, where he purchased certain gifts, suddenly he saw Dimitri.

"What are you doing here?" asked Giora surprised.

"I am waiting for you" said Dimitri.

"I guess you still have your pass to enter this area of transit flights" said Giora.

"We haven't got much time, so listen carefully", he whispered. Giora could feel his unusual anxiety, not typical of the Dimitri he knew.

"You have a dangerous sleeper in your organization! It will complete astonish everybody."

"Who? How do you know and why now?" asked Giora.

"About who, it will cost you, about how I know, I have solid proof supported by authentic original documents. This is very hot recent info. I spent plenty of time in a special location of the former KGB top secret archive that was revealed just recently. I had special info and sold it to CIA and to MI6, they liked it... otherwise they wouldn't pay."

"Listen" said Giora, "You know how it works, I can't go back only with your general words and they will fill in your Swiss account."

Dimitri opened his case and handed Giora one page. It was quite yellow and looked like it was typed with an ancient typewriter.

"You can take this for free. I have the rest.

I am sure you know what it means," said Dimitri.

Giora felt like he was holding an explosive in his hand. The subject was about Russian *assets* in Israel. He had already seen a similar document in the past, so he knew what to expect to be on the following pages.

One of the documents he had seen was related to the Marcus Klingberg affair.

Abraham Marcus Klingberg was the highest ranking Soviet spy ever caught in Israel. Fearing the Nazis in World War II, he escaped from Poland to the USSR, where he finished his medical studies.

He served as medical officer in the Red Army and in 1948 he immigrated to Israel, where he served in the Medical Corps of the IDF. In 1957 he joined the top-secret Israel Institute for Biological Research (IIBR) in Ness Ziona, where he served as Deputy Scientific Director. Klingberg had actually started his espionage activity in the 1950s. Israel's foreign and domestic intelligence agencies, the Mossad and Shin-Bet, began to suspect Klingberg of espionage.

In January 1983 Shin-Bet officers informed Klingberg they wanted to send him to Singapore where a chemical plant had blown up. On his way to the airport he was taken to an undisclosed location where he was interrogated. Klingberg confessed and claimed that the information that he provided to the Soviet Union was for ideological reasons only. He was found guilty of passing secrets to the Soviet Union and sentenced to twenty years in prison.

However, very few knew that the vital information about Klingberg's activity came from the collapsing Soviet Union KGB's archive.

"OK, I'll make the contact", said Giora.

"That's not good enough. You know I trust you, but I need to know that you'll support this and that I'll get my money. These are difficult times and I have no retirement funds from the KGB..." said Dimitri sarcastically.

Dimitri trusted nobody, but he had a special relationship with Giora, who had saved his life during an unusual event in Hong-Kong in the late 70s.

"I'll do my best," promised Giora while tapping Dimitri's shoulder.

"Yoptfoyomat!" cursed Giora so Dimitri could understand when he realized that he was going to miss the flight. He saw the plane through the glass window leaving the hub slowly to the runway.

"Don't worry," said Dimitri, who made a phone call.

"Come with me," he said while turning quickly toward the exit.

They left the Duty-Free area and ran toward the exit of the building. With his extensive experience Giora thought for a moment that it might be a setup of some kind. At the gates a military jeep arrived and they climbed into it. They drove around the building entering through a security zone into the runway. Giora saw the plane stopped and a special stairway was pulled next to the plane door.

"Do Svidaniya", said Dimitri and added, "I'll never forget Hong-Kong"...

16. The Iranian Nuclear Threats.

IRAN HAS BEEN PART OF JEWISH HISTORY since Biblical times. The biblical books of Ezra, Nehemiah, and Esther tell the story, the life and experiences of Jews in Persia.

From the establishment of the State of Israel in 1948 until the Iranian Revolution in 1979, Israel and Iran maintained quite a close relationship. Their military links and projects were kept secret. They had also been cooperating in development of a joint missile project.

Ahmadinejad was elected President in August 2005. Since then, he has constantly attacked Israel and its right to exist. He was quoted as saying. "Israel regime must be wiped off the map." The Iranian attempt to develop nuclear capabilities in conjunction with the threats of the current regime has led Israel to warn Iran that it is prepared to take unilateral military action. Israel will take such an action provided the international community fails to stop the development of Iranian capabilities to develop nuclear weapons.

In 2005 Israeli Prime Minister Ariel Sharon gave the green light for IDF's Special Forces to plan for possible strikes on uranium enrichment sites in Iran.

The U.S. Department of Defense is aware of that option and they are cooperating with the Israelis on this issue.

There is a secret Israeli plan to strike Iranian nuclear enrichment facilities at Natanz. It might be executed using special nuclear bunker busters developed by Israel.

Those penetrating bombs are much more effective than the American GBU-39 standoff bunker penetrating bombs which the Bush administration sold to Israel.

It could be done by one strike and the Iranian nuclear project would be wiped out.

A declassified secret CIA document from October 1994 deals with Iran's pattern of assassination.

Iran's policy of assassinating oppositionists has changed little under President Ali Hashemi Rafsanjani.

The number of assassinations conducted by Iran has stayed roughly constant during Rafanjani's tenure. Since 1989, Iran has carried out an average of five assassinations annually, and groups supported by Tehran particularly radical Turkish Islamists, average another two killings annually.

Key targets have remained largely unchanged during Rafanjani's tenure. Most Iranian assassination targets are members of the Mojahedine Khalq or the Kurdish Democratic Party of Iran (KDP-I). Iran attacks these two groups much more frequently than the third key Iranian target, supporters of the son of the former Shah of Iran.

Some specific targets have changed to adapt to alterations in Iranian foreign policy, Saudi diplomats were attacked during 1989 and 1990, shortly after Saudi Arabia executed the Kuwait Shia responsible for bombings at the Hajj in 1989 but have not been targeted since. Iran rarely relies on surrogates to conduct assassinations of Iranians oppositionists.

Iran typically relies on surrogates for attacks on non-Iranians. Turkish Islamic groups supported by Iran, for example, is responsible for killing a handful of secular Turkish journalists and a Member of Parliament since 1989.

In addition, attacks on foreigners in Turkey, including the attempted murder of Jewish businessman Jak Kamhi (1993) and the bombings that killed U.S. serviceman Victor Marvick (l991) and Israeli security officer Ehud Sadan {1992), have been linked to Islamic groups backed by Iran.

Although the pace and targets of Iranian assassinations are not changing significantly, a review of killings since 1989 suggests that Iran is killing fewer oppositionists in Europe and more in Southwest Asia, particularly Turkey and Iraq.

We suspect this change results from Iran's interest in protecting its diplomatic and economic initiatives in Europe.

We note that the drop in assassinations in Europe began in 1993, when Iran began experiencing difficulties in repaying foreign loans and the United States increased pressure on European countries to halt credits to Iran. Countries surrounding Iran particularly Turkey, Iraq, and Pakistan, offer a wealth of targets, and killings in those countries result in less diplomatic backlash for Iran than assassinations in Europe. Despite the apparent shift from Europe and the increased focus on assassinations in Southwest Asia, we have noted several suspicious murders of oppositionists in Europe during the past year.

We cannot confirm that they were carried out by Iran, and we have not included them in our statistics. These attacks include: 17 January 1994. Bagarmossen, Sweden. A member of the KDP-I was severely injured by a letter-bomb addressed to his wife, also a KDP-I member, according to defense attaché reporting. 11 October 1994. Oslo, Norway. William Nygaard, Norwegian publisher of Salman Rushdie's novel, The Satanic Verses, was shot near his home.

The Iranian threats with their aggressive attempts to develop nuclear weapons have forced Israel to prepare for preemptive action.

There have been many signs, public and covert, that Israel is and has been conducting exercises for such an act. One of those exercises, according to certain sources, was the landing attempts in Budapest airport by two civilian planes in March 2010.

Another source claims that the secret plan is to generate a diversion near the main target in Iran by such civilian planes while at the same time the military bombers will hit the target. The distance from Israel to Iran is somewhat less than from Israel to Hungary...

17. Islamic Invasion into Democratic Societies.

The worldwide Islamic invasion was envisioned by Nostradamus in the mid-1500s. Among other prophesies, he described Anti-Christian Moslem forces in Iraq and Syria, persecution in the Moslem countries of Asia, especially in Turkey. From Israel the war extends to Western Europe and there will be a Third World War using nuclear missiles...

In his prophesies, Nostradamus described the Islamic demographic movement or invasion into Europe. This prophesy of invasion has become a reality.

During the period of 1990-2010 there has been a significant demographic change in most European countries. The natural immigration from Islamic countries into Europe has significantly increased the size of the Moslem minorities in those countries.

Muslims struggle to convert the world to Islam. In the past Christianity and Islam wanted to spread the word to everybody everywhere and by force if necessary.

Today Christians and other religions no longer wish to conquer and use force in the name of their faith; however, Muslims do.

In the era of politically correctness in Europe and the U.S., this invasion is generally ignored in the name of multiculturalism. Muslims even have a right-wing acceptance and support by anti-Jewish elements in Europe.

Time is working in favor of the Moslem minorities. While Europe becomes older, the Moslem communities will develop into the majority as their demographic increase is about three times greater than the indigenous Europeans'. Yet another prophesy of Nostradamus is fulfilled.

There are those who don't believe in prophecies in general and particularly not those written in riddles which may have multiple interpretations.

However, when one considers the many prophecies that have proven correct, it is rather difficult to dismiss them as nonsense.

La grande bande et secte crucigere,
Se dressera en Mésopotamie:
Du proche fleuve compagnie lege,
Que telle loy tiendra pour ennemie. [CIII,Q61]

The great band and anti-Christian sect of Moslems will rise up in Iraq and Syria near the Euphrates with a tank force and will hold the [Christian] law to be its enemy. This particular interpretation was by Jean-Charles de Fontbrune, translated by Alexis Lykiard, printed back in 1984. A later interpretation was:

The great host and sect of the crusaders,
Will be massed in Mesopotamia:
Of the nearby river the fast company,
That such law will hold for the enemy.

In the midst of the first Gulf war about the end of 1990, while sitting in the specially prepared "safe" room for protection against conventional and chemical warfare, Giora finalized his license agreement with the Israel Aerospace Industries (IAI) for the marketing of his neurological monitor, the Neuritor™.

Giora took the military instructions for the civilians quite seriously. When the first scud missile fell on Israel, he donned his gas mask like everyone else and waited for instruction from the civil guard. .

The most difficult part of this war was to observe the eyes of his frightened daughters wearing the mask.

In his mind, seeing himself sitting in the "safe" room, hugging his daughters during the loud siren alarm was a very painful picture.

However, when his daughters were not visiting, he was not so anxious to put on his gas mask, especially when several friends were with him in the safe room.

During that period numerous political views were exchanged among the friends in the safe room.

"The Americans are doing a great job in destroying Iraqi forces," said Giora and added, "However they will pay a high price eventually".

"What do you mean?" he was asked.

"Well, they definitely will win the war, but what will be after they win?"

"There will be elections and Iraq will become a Democracy," was the answer, followed by few laughs.

"You forget Iraq's neighbors," said Giora.

"What about the neighbors?"

"They are pro-Iranian or afraid of them. A military victory will not generate a stable Democracy in the region without the consent of the neighbors and they don't want or can't have a Democratic Iraq," said Giora.

An interesting CIA document written in July 1970 that was classified "Top Secret" was approved for release on 16th of September 2009.

Its title was "The Clandestine Introduction of Nuclear Weapons into the US."

The problem was "to asses the capabilities of foreign nations to introduce nuclear weapons into the U.S. and to estimate the likelihood of such introduction over the next few years."

Further quoting from that document:

Leaders of any nation would have to weigh any possible advantages against the grave consequences which would follow from discovery. Despite all precautions there would always be risk of detection arising not only from U.S. security measures, but also from the chance of U.S. penetration of the clandestine apparatus, the defection of an agent, or sheer accident.

The enemy leaders would almost certainly judge that use of this tactic would be regarded by the U.S. as a warlike act, if not as a cause for war, and that it would precipitate an international political crisis of the first magnitude.

The estimate is that no nation would consider this course except possibly in the context of planning an attack on the US, of deterring the U.S. from an attack on itself, or conceivably as an act of deception designed to embroil the U.S. with a third power. Only four foreign nations-the USSR, the UK, France and Communist China-have developed and tested nuclear weapons.

Beyond these, only India and Israel may do so over the next several years. The CIA *can foresee no changes in the world situation so radical as to motivate the UK, France or any of the potential nuclear powers to attempt to clandestinely introduce nuclear weapons into the US. For this reason they were concerned only with the Soviet Union and Communist China.*

The CIA further analyzed such possibilities in detail.

Nuclear weapons with weights of up to a few thousand pounds could be brought across U.S. borders by common means of transport without great difficulty but not without some risk.

The difficulties and risks of introducing larger weapons into the US, even in a disassembled state, are probably sufficiently great to seriously discourage such attempts.

Such devices could be carried in by fishing boats or similar small craft to which transfer had been made at sea. Any weapon could be brought into U.S. waters in merchant ships and detonated without removal from the ship.

According to the CIA of the 1970s, the Soviet Intelligence services assigned high priority to the development of espionage and sabotage capabilities in the U.S. and presumably formed an organization for the latter purpose.

This top secret document was distributed to the White House, National Security Council, Department of State, Department of Defense, Atomic Energy Commission and the Federal Bureau of Investigation.We all are lucky that this scenario is still on paper and hopefully it will remain there.

An interesting document about the growth in population from 2000 to 2015, or "Global Trends 2015," was prepared under the direction of the National Intelligence Council in December 2000. It was approved for publication by the National Foreign Intelligence Board under the authority of the Director of the Central Intelligence.

The Middle East and North Africa play a significant role in that document.

Regimes in the region from Morocco to Iran will have to cope with demographic, economic and societal pressures from within aid globalization from without.

No single ideology or philosophy will unite any one state or group of states in response to these challenges, although popular resentment of globalization as a Western intrusion will be widespread. Political Islam in various forms will be an attractive alternative for millions of Muslims throughout the region, and some radical variants will continue to be divisive social and political forces.

By 2015, Israel will have attained a cold peace with its neighbors, with only limited social, economic, and cultural ties.

There will be a Palestinian state, but Israeli-Palestinian tensions will persist and occasionally erupt into crises. Old rivalries among core states: Egypt, Syria, Iraq, and Iran, will reemerge.

International attention will shift anew to the Persian Gulf an increasingly important source of energy resources to fuel the global economy, and oil revenues anticipated for Iraq, Iran, and Saudi Arabia in particular will provide strategic and potentially destabilizing options for those states.

New relationships between geographic regions could emerge between North Africa and Europe (on trade); India China and the Persian Gulf (on energy); and Israel Turkey and India (on economic, technical and in the case of Turkey, security considerations).

A key driver for the Middle East over the next 15 years will be demographic pressures, specifically how to provide jobs, housing, public services, and subsidies for rapidly growing and increasingly urban populations. By 2015, in much of the Middle East populations will be significantly larger, poorer, more urban, and more disillusioned.

In nearly all Middle Eastern countries, more than half the population is now under 20 years of age. These populations will continue to have very large youth cohorts through 2015, with the labor force growing at an average rate of 3.1 percent per year. The problem of job placement is compounded by weak educational systems producing a generation lacking the technical and problem-solving skills required for economic growth.

With the exception of Israel, Middle Eastern states will view globalization more as a challenge than an opportunity.

Although the Internet will remain confined to a small elite due to relatively high cost, undeveloped infrastructures, and cultural obstacles, the information revolution and other technological advances probably will have a net destabilizing effect on the Middle East by raising expectations, increasing income disparities, and eroding the power of regimes to control information or mold popular opinion.

Attracting foreign direct investment will also be difficult: except for the energy sector, investors will tend to shy away from these countries, discouraged by overbearing state sectors; heavy, opaque, and arbitrary government regulation; underdeveloped financial sectors; inadequate physical infrastructure; and the threat of political instability.

Most Middle Eastern governments recognize the need for economic restructuring and even a modicum of greater political participation, but they will proceed cautiously, fearful of undermining their rule.

As some governments or sectors embrace the new economy and civil society while others cling to more traditional paradigms, inequities between and within states will grow.

Islamists could come to power in states that are beginning to become pluralist and in which entrenched secular elites have lost their appeal.

This document predicts certain demographic changes, which should concern Israel. The concern should not only be about the expected demographic changes among Israel's neighbors, but the changes within Israel as well.

The rapidly increasing Israeli Palestinian population is likely to increase their part in the Israeli government.

They will continue to be a minority but with increasing power every year.

Another sector that has a high birthrate is the Jewish religious orthodox groups. On one hand this is a blessed increase in population; on the other hand, it will change Israel's governing structure with significant power going to the religious groups. The problem foreseen is in several areas. As some of the orthodox people do not work but study, it will affect the Israel tax payer and the division of the "economic pie."

Moreover, some of the religious groups do not serve in the army, which not only generates a burden on those who serve three years, but it is demoralizing as well.

Over the years, Israel has faced many difficulties in integrating newcomers from so many countries and cultures. The US is facing similar problems. The need for low skilled and cheap labor exists and there is a needed to fill this demand. The problem then is not one of numbers, skill, legality, national origin or labor needs, but rather one of integration.

Jews in the US are a minority and they have made a substantial contribution to the US economy, science and culture. They are minority in everywhere except in Israel.

Here it would be appropriate to tell a joke about the Rabbi and the Priest… In a small town somewhere there one Priest and one Rabbi served their congregations.

They had grown up in that town and were friends. On many occasions they allowed themselves to criticize each other and they occasionally presented provocative questions and scenarios to each other.

During one of such cases of debate, the Priest said to the Rabbi, "You are always telling us about the problems in Israel, which I simply cannot understand.

While you, the Jews in this country are very resourceful and successful as lawyers, bankers and scientists, how come you can't resolve your problems in Israel?"

The Rabbi replied: "You see, we the Jews are like fertilizers. When we are spread we generate wealth and growth, but when we are together in a pile, we stink…"

Golda Meir told President Nixon, "You are the president of 150 million Americans; I am the prime minister of six million prime ministers."

Apart from those and other jokes and comments about Jews, sometimes on the verge of anti-Semitism, maintaining the unique and the only democracy in the Middle East and ruling and managing Jews in Israel is not an easy task.

Although, the people of Israel promised God at Sinai: "Naaseh V'Nishma"…, "We will do first, and afterwards, understand" (Shemot/Exodus 24:7), these days it is difficult to follow the leaders and agree with their policy and views when there are so many different opinions.

Some will argue that multi-views in a multi-pluralistic society are an advantage to reaching the right decisions. However, in many cases a multiplicity of views may put obstacles in the way of reaching democratic ways and goals.

"We the people" will change our opinion according to the current situation, influenced by emotion and many other distracting factors. Polls taken eight, or four months or a week prior to election may be significantly different; mob views can be manipulated.

These days the media plays a major role in influencing the opinions of the individual who usually bases decisions only on the information from the media. The media can be manipulated.

Major players or companies in a Democratic-Capitalistic society often will adopt the statement, "Ask not what is good for the country, ask what is good for the company." It's not that they don't care about the country, but in case of conflicting interests they will put their company in front. A similar scenario exists in Israel under the category of "Hon-Shilton" or "Wealth-Government" relationships.

According to Business Data Israel (BDI) and other sources, there are 15-19 families in Israel whose income is about 34% of the leading 500 companies, which is equivalent to 88% from the government's annual budget. Such a centralization of wealth and its close relationship to certain individuals in the government is generating unhealthy and undesired situations.

Typical of such situations is a government official who is a decision maker with regard to one of the companies. When he retires, sometimes early, he goes to work for the same company or for the family controlling that company.

The following is a citation from the *Journal of Economic Literature* (Vol. 43, No. 3, September 2005), entitled: "Corporate Governance, Economic Entrenchment, and Growth", by Randall Morck, Daniel Wolfenzon and Bernard Yeung.

Outside the United States and the United Kingdom, large corporations usually have controlling owners, who are usually very wealthy families.

Pyramidal control structures, cross shareholding, and super-voting rights let such families control corporations without making a commensurate capital investment.

In many countries, a few such families end up controlling considerable proportions of their countries' economies. Three points emerge. First, at the firm level, these ownership structures, because they vest dominant control rights with families who often have little real capital invested, permit a range of agency problems and hence resource misallocation.

If a few families control large swaths of an economy, such corporate governance problems can attain macroeconomic importance-affecting rates of innovation, economy wide resource allocation, and economic growth.

If political influence depends on what one controls, rather than what one owns, the controlling owners of pyramids have greatly amplified political influence relative to their actual wealth.

This influence can distort public policy regarding property rights protection, capital markets, and other institutions.

We denote this phenomenon economic entrenchment, and posit a relationship between the distribution of corporate control and institutional development that generates and preserves economic entrenchment as one possible equilibrium.

Due to the expected demographic changes predicted above, the Israeli people via their democratically elected leaders must take that into consideration.

Israel is a diverse nation that successfully absorbed new immigrants from more than 140 countries. Among its population there are about 1.5 million Arabs who are represented in the Israeli Knesset.

There are many types of democracies. The following is a partial list:

Constitutional democracy - This is a democracy that is governed by a constitution.

Defensive democracy - This is a type of democracy where there is a need to limit certain rights, even freedom in order protect institutions of the democracy.

Religious democracy - A type of democracy where the religion is in the center of the public arena.

Parliamentary democracy - A democracy where the cabinet, which is the executive branch of a parliamentary government, is headed by a prime minister.

Multiparty democracy - Multiple political parties may gain control of government usually in a coalition.

A dictator is a ruler whose powers are unconstrained by external or superior law. The dictator is the law, so he can take whatever actions he wants even if they are considered to be illegal.

"Can we have a combination of two different ruling systems?" The answer is yes; it is a very interesting type of democracy called *Democratic dictatorship.*

Democratic elections will place a dictator into a position of power.

After he assumes office, the dictator will use the extensive powers that he is able to exercise. So, it is entirely possible to have a democratically elected dictator. He will be duly elected to office and will be able to exercise dictatorial powers.

Israel is a *multiparty parliamentary democracy*. Basic laws enumerate fundamental rights. The 120 members of the Knesset have the power to dissolve the Government and mandate elections. Actually, if we look carefully, we may see some other features from all the abovementioned democracies embedded in the evolving and adapting Israeli multiparty parliamentary democracy.

Israel needs strong and decisive leaders who can take risks for the benefit of the country and not for the benefit of the party.

Israel is not like other nations. The existence of Israel is not justified by insuring the welfare of its citizens alone; it has, in addition, special ideological and ancient roots and beliefs that not only unite the people of Israel but justify their existence in Eretz Israel, the historical homeland of the Jewish people.

עם ישראל תלוי בארץ ישראל השייך לעם ישראל,
כפי שהבטיח האלוהים לאברהם (בראשית יז-8):

"וְנָתַתִּי לְךָ וּלְזַרְעֲךָ אַחֲרֶיךָ אֵת אֶרֶץ מְגֻרֶיךָ,
אֵת כָּל-אֶרֶץ כְּנַעַן, לַאֲחֻזַּת עוֹלָם; וְהָיִיתִי לָהֶם לֵאלֹהִים"

*The land of Israel belongs to the People of Israel,
so promised God to Abraham. (Genesis 17:8)*

*"And I will give unto thee,
and to thy seed after thee,
the land wherein thou art a stranger,
all the land of Canaan,
for an everlasting possession;
and I will be their God"*

18. Closure at Mike's Funeral.

AT MIKE'S FUNERAL, Giora felt like he had lost a close relative. He saw Mike's family with red eyes mourning the loss of their loved one. After the funeral Rafi asked Giora to join him and while they sat in the back of Rafi's car, Rafi asked his driver to leave them alone and take a walk. Rafi had replaced Gadi, who retired from service and went back to his farm in Northern Galilee.

"You should know that Mike committed suicide," said Rafi quietly.

"What!?" cried Giora.

"Actually, you had something to do with it."

"What are you talking about? You know I don't like such riddles or jokes," said Giora angrily. "Mike and his family were Russian agents. He was retrained and became active after his father died in 1963. We never ever suspected him. After you gave us Dimitri's document, we started to connect the dots. We paid Dimitri well and he gave us not only Mike but two other non-important sleepers as well."

"My God," said Giora quietly. "So Dimitri was right."

"Yes he was," said Rafi and added, "We called for a meeting at Mike's office as usual.

We thought that this way he wouldn't suspect what was coming. I gave him the documents without saying anything."

"What was his reaction?"

"He asked his secretary for a cup of tea and coffee for us. He opened his drawer and poured some brandy into his tea as he usually did, but this time it was not brandy. He knew that we were on to him and drank the poison in front of us; he was prepared."

"What poison? What drug did he take?"

"As you know he was quite expert in his field and had access to our labs. He took Scoline, also known as Suxamethonium, which as you know is normally used in anesthesia. He took a lethal dosage."

Suxamethonium is a white crystalline odorless substance, highly soluble in water. It paralyzes the capacity to supply oxygen, remove carbon dioxide, eventually leading to circulatory collapse and death.

"You could have saved him," said Giora.

"Yes we could have, but he specifically asked not to try and leave him alone in his office, which we did."

"What about his family?"

"We told his family that he had a heart attack and died immediately; we made sure it went smoothly and arranged for a quick funeral without the possibility of an undesired autopsy."

"He asked us to let him go this way and begged that we leave his family alone because they were not involved at all. After careful consideration, we decided to close this case and bury it with him. His family knows nothing and as you know his wife died six years ago."

"Did he say anything before he died?"

"He said that he had stopped cooperating with the Russians after five years. He asked me to tell you that he was sorry and hoped you could forgive him."

Giora felt that it was not the whole story.

"You do have more. I can feel it," said Giora.

"You still have your sharp senses," smiled Rafi.

"His original name was Michael Weisz.
Does it ring a bell?"
It took Giora a while to recognize the name.
"Oh my God," I thought I knew Mike.

After WWII, the Russians had made a special effort to recruit special agents and due to the changing political situations they planted sleeper-assets in the USA and its allies, especially in Israel. The Kleins had been recruited in Hungary, their Uncle Leo was known in the KGB as "Leonid the recruiter." He tried to train Pista, Klein's son but he was a moron. Leo found what he needed in Michael, son of Ilona Weisz. He arranged for their visa after their capture trying to escape from Hungary in 1949. The Russians had tried to transfer them within a group of illegal immigrants but they failed.

"You know the rest of the story," Rafi said.

"Yes I know," said Giora.

"He betrayed our country, I would have killed him myself if he had not committed suicide."

19. Epilogue.

THIS BOOK is going to print when Dr. Giora Ram is in the right age to start summarizing and exposing an eventful life for the knowledge of the next generation.

Certain events told might raise some eyebrows, especially within his family. They probably will connect the dots reading this book, realizing that they were part of his unusual worldwide adventures without knowing it.

If one would contact the appropriate Israeli authority such as the Israeli Military Intelligence Censor (see their authorization stamp on the back cover of this book) or the Mossad spokesman and ask about Dr. Ram and to comment about his book, the answer would probably be: "No one by that name was ever employed by us." or "We do not have and never had any *Unit* or *Room* as described in his book" or "We have no knowledge of such a person in our organization, not ever."

"What about the implied events?"

"Some happened and some did not," would be the answer.

Giora is a world traveler, who has visited many places, especially those where tourists rarely go. His adventures have taken him to dark alleys, remote deserts and to unusual locations and situations.

He was almost killed on many occasions, such as at the ski resort in Marilleva in the north eastern part of Italy. This location, at a height of 1400 meters, has slopes which offer various skiing options, both for regular and advanced skiers. He has fought with muggers in Bangkok and in Manhattan.

Giora has published many scientific and philosophical articles and he is the author of eleven books, five in English and six in Hebrew (Amazon). He speaks Hungarian, Hebrew, English and German. Giora is divorced and has three children.

Dr. Giora Ram is living now in Israel

He is still very active…

20. CIA Documents.

DIRECTORATE OF
SCIENCE & TECHNOLOGY

Scientific and Technical
Intelligence Report

*Free-World Sounding Rockets, Ballistic Missiles,
and Satellite Launch Vehicles*

ARCHIVAL RECORD
PLEASE RETURN TO
AGENCY ARCHIVES, BLDG.

Secret
FMSAC-STIR/69-1
February 1969

Copy Nº 41

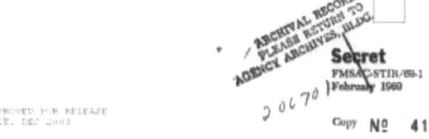

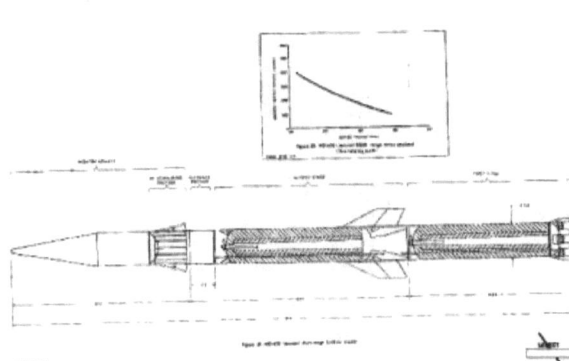

21. References and Pictures.

Khazaria map from 600 - 850 CE

Weiser Fülöp   Weiser Alex-Shlomo

Esther – 1934   Alex&Esther-1945

Rachel & Gyuri-1947   Rachel-1954

Yitzhak Rabin, IDF-Chief of Staff & Dov Ram – 1967

Rafael Eitan (Raful), IDF-Chief of Staff

Receiving the rank of Brigadier General - 1979
(U.S. navy equivalent to Rear-Admiral or Commodore
in the U.K.)

With PM Yitzhak Shamir

With PM Ariel Sharon

With PM Shimon Peres

22. Censorship.

This page represents all the paragraphs in this book that were deleted to protect Israel's national security.

Beatae vitae consequuntur dicta sunt explicabo. Nemo enim ipsam voluptatem quia voluptas sit.

There are many *non-existing* government facilities, such as: Aspernatur odit, aut fugit, sed quia magni, ratione sequi, voluptatem and nesciunt.

Dimona for some years was only a small part of the "real-thing", which is conducted elsewhere... at *non-existing* government facilities.

Neque porro 504 quisquam est, qui dolorem 8200 ipsum quia dolor sit amet, adipisci velit, sed quia non numquam eius modi consectetur 8513 incidunt ut labore et dolore.

The nuclear war-heads ready to be launched simultaneously to selected targets are located at yet another *non-existing* facility deep down at:

Magnam voluptatem, enim minima, quis nostrum veniam, exercitationem, ullam aliquam, quaerat suscipit and corporis laboriosam tempora...

23. Reader's Response.

A LETTER DATED January 12, 2011 from The President of the State of Israel, Mr. Shimon Peres. (First edition was titled: "The Hungarian Connection")

נשיא המדינה

ירושלים, ז' בשבט תשע"א
12 בינואר 2011

לכבוד
ד"ר גיורא רם
ת.ד. 11206
תל אביב 61111

גיורא היקר,

ברצוני להודות לך על ספרך "The Hungarian Connection" אשר שלחת אליי.

ספרך שוזר בעניין רב את סיפור חייך הסוערים לצד ניתוחים של התרחשויות ואירועים היסטוריים, אשר אודות חלקם רב עדיין הנסתר על הגלוי.

בברכת המשך עשייה פורה ויישר כוח.

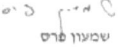

שמעון פרס

"Your book intertwines with a great deal the story of your turbulent life alongside analyses of historical events, some of which are still unknown and secret."

229

A letter dated September 11, 2011 from The Prime
Minister of the State of Israel, Mr. Benjamin Netanyahu.

ראש הממשלה
Prime Minister

ירושלים, י"ב באלול התשע"א
11 בספטמבר 2011
סימוכין : 76767

לכבוד
ד"ר גיורא רם
ת.ד 11206
<u>תל אביב - יפו</u>

גיורא שלום,

קיבלתי בשמחה את ספרך האוטוביוגרפי "הקשר ההונגרי"

סיפרך, המגולל את סיפור חייך בשילוב עם אירועים היסטוריים, מלמד על
סיפור חיים מסעיר ויוצא דופן, ועל אהבה אמיתית למדינת ישראל.

אני מעריך מאוד את פנייתך ומודה לך על הספר.

ב ב ר כ ה ,

בנימין נתניהו

Jerusalem, Israel

(First edition was titled: "The Hungarian Connection")
"Your book, which tells the story of your life in
combination with historical events, teaches about an
exciting and unusual life story and true love for
the State of Israel."

24. Books by Dr. Giora Ram (English):

Nuke Them Till Eternity (prev. **The Hungarian Connection**)
An Autobiographical Novel.
Published in Israel by IMEXCO General Ltd, 2010, 2018
ISBN 978-965-91623-9-0 | Paperback and Kindle formats on Amazon
http://nuke.imexco.com

Sex and Scientific Philosophy
A unique collection of earthly and heavenly questions arising
during our intellectual evolution.
Published in Israel by IMEXCO General Ltd, 2012
ISBN 978-965-91623-1-4 | Paperback and Kindle formats on Amazon
http://philosex.imexco.com

**Hunting for Antiques and Collectables: The Adventures of an
Antique Collector**
Hunting adventures for unique and rare antiques and collectables
Published in Israel by IMEXCO General Ltd, 2013
ISBN 978-965-91623-2-1 | Paperback and Kindle formats on Amazon
http://aoc.imexco.com ; http://antiques.imexco.com

Evolutionary and Philosophical Insights into Global Education
This book is in two parts. In part one, the focus is on past and
present educational methods and systems whilst part two contains
forward-looking views and opinions on educational needs and
possible new forms of information transfer.
Published in Israel by IMEXCO General Ltd, 2015
ISBN 978-965-91623-3-8 | Paperback and Kindle formats on Amazon
http://edu.imexco.com

Education and Alternative Treatments for ADHD
A unique methodological non-drug-based treatment successfully
implemented on the author's son is presented here in conjunction
with global education related issues.
Published in Israel by IMEXCO General Ltd, 2015
ISBN 978-965-91623-6-9 | Paperback and Kindle formats on Amazon
http://adhd.imexco.com

Articles in English
https://ezinearticles.com/expert/Dr_Giora_Ram/1368314

Books by Dr. Giora Ram (Hebrew):

ADHD - Children of Tomorrow
A unique co-production of a special child and his father.
Published in Israel by Gvanim, 2010
DanaCode 00860000644-6 | Paperback and Kindle formats on Amazon
http://adhd.imexco.com

The House on the Hill
Poems and Love Letters
Published in Israel by IMEXCO General Ltd, 2010
DanaCode 08000250081-4 | Paperback and Kindle formats on Amazon
http://love-u.imexco.com

My Love, My Wife, My Divorcee
Dating and mating
Published in Israel by IMEXCO General Ltd, 2010
DanaCode 08000250082-1 | Paperback and Kindle formats on Amazon
http://my-love.imexco.com

Mr. Giggle the Story Teller
Adventures in the world of dreams
Published in Israel by IMEXCO General Ltd, 2016
ISBN 978-965-91623-5-2 | Paperback and Kindle formats on Amazon
http://mrgiggle.imexco.com

A Tale of Love and Passion for Life
What would a retired Mossad agent do when he discovers that he
has a terminal cancer and has only three more months left to live?
This novel is based on the turbulent exciting life of a Mossad agent.
Published in Israel by IMEXCO General Ltd, 2016
ISBN 978-965-91623-4-5 | Paperback format on Amazon
http://passion4life.imexco.com

Stories and Poems about Love and Life
This book contains a collection of short stories written by the author
during the last decade. They were published in various media, blogs
and appeared in books written by the author.
Published in Israel by Dr. Giora Ram, 2017
ISBN 978-965-91623-7-6 | Paperback format on Amazon
http://stories.imexco.com

Articles in Hebrew
https://www.articles.co.il/authorFB/28455